The Last Word

✪ ✪ ✪

"Bodine, I want you to help the newspaper editor here pick up his type."

There was a collective gasp of surprise from the onlookers as they heard Sam's strange request.

"I don't plan to tell you again," Sam said. His words were soft and cajoling. And yet it was that cold, emotionless tone that made the words frightening. "Pick up the newspaperman's type."

"Slater, you got more nerve and less sense than anyone I ever saw," Bodine said. He moved the pistol so that it pointed at Sam. "Don't you see that I got the drop on you? All I got to do is pull the trigger."

Sam shook his head slowly. "No," he said. "You may try to pull the trigger, but I'll kill you before you can get the job done. Pick up the type, Bodine, or die with the gun in your hand."

Also by Dale Colter

The Regulator
Diablo at Daybreak
Deadly Justice
Dead Man's Ride
Gravedancer
The Scalp Hunters
Paradise Mountain
Desert Pursuit
Montana Showdown
Payback
Trail of Death

Published by
HARPERPAPERBACKS

THE REGULATOR

✪ SLAUGHTER AT PUXICO ✪

DALE COLTER

HarperPaperbacks
A Division of HarperCollinsPublishers

HarperPaperbacks *A Division of* HarperCollins*Publishers*
          10 East 53rd Street, New York, N.Y. 10022

Cover illustration by Miro Sinovcic

First printing: May 1994

Printed in the United States of America

HarperPaperbacks and colophon are trademarks of
HarperCollins*Publishers*

❖ 10 9 8 7 6 5 4 3 2 1

CHAPTER 1

THE LITTLE TOWN WAS HOT, DRY, AND DUSTY. It had grown up in the middle of nowhere and now sat baking in the sun like a lizard. To the three riders approaching from the west, the collection of adobe and sun-bleached wooden buildings were so much a part of the land that it looked almost as if the town were the result of some natural phenomenon, rather than the work of man.

Out on the edge of the town its civic-minded citizens had erected a sign which read:

SUNDOWN
POPULATION 412
FRIENDLY, INDUSTRIOUS, PROGRESSIVE
COME GROW WITH US

Terry Estes, the youngest of the three riders, slipped his canteen off the pommel and took a drink. The water was tepid, but his tongue was dry and swollen. He wiped the back of his hand across his mouth, then recorked the canteen and hung it back on his saddle.

"Don't you think, maybe, we could stop at a saloon and get us a few beers afore we take care of our business?" he asked. "It's goin' to take a beer to wet this dryness."

"You just had a drink of water," Billy Lobo answered.

"Yeah, but this water's beginnin' to taste like piss."

"We ain't goin' into no saloons in this town," Billy said. Billy Lobo was the leader of the three. He was also the oldest, though he was only twenty-one.

"If we start drinkin' with the locals, then the next thing you know, ever'one's goin' to have a good description of us."

"Hell, Billy," Johnny Singleton said. "You think they ain't goin' to have a good description of us anyway, the moment we rob that bank of their'n?" He hawked up a spit. "Lookee there," he added. "I ain't got enough wet to even spit proper."

"They ain't goin' to recognize us if we do this job right," Billy ordered. "If you do just like I tell you, we'll be into that bank, have the money, and then be out of here again afore anyone in this town knows what hit 'em." He smiled at the other two. "Then when we ride into the next town we can go in in style. We'll have enough to swim in beer if we want to. Women, hotels, restaurants, some gamblin' money . . . hell, we can do anything we want."

"You ever know'd anyone to get 'im two whores at the same time?" Terry asked.

Johnny laughed. "Two whores? Hell, you ain't never had one yet, have you?" he asked.

"Why, sure I have, lots of times," Terry insisted. "Whenever I got the money, that is, which, most of the time, I don't have."

"Well, you just do what I tell you to today, and you'll have all the money you need . . . even enough for two whores at the same time if you think you can handle that," Billy said. "Now, let's get on with it. You two boys, check your pistols."

The three men pulled their pistols and checked the cylinders to see that all the chambers were properly charged. Then they slipped their guns back into their holsters.

"Ready?" Billy asked.

"Ready," Terry replied.

Johnny nodded in the affirmative.

The three men rode on into town, then pulled up in front of the small bank. Billy and Johnny dismounted and handed their reins to Terry. Terry remained in the saddle and kept his eyes open on the street out front. Billy and Johnny looked up and down the street once, then they pulled their kerchiefs up over the bottom half of their faces and, with their guns drawn, pushed open the door.

There were three customers in the bank when Billy and Johnny rushed in. Because of the masks on the robbers' faces and the guns in their hands, the customers and the bank teller knew, immediately, what was going on.

"You fellas! Get your hands up and stand over against the wall!" Billy shouted to the three customers.

The three customers complied with the orders.

Billy hopped over the railing to go behind the teller cage, then held his sack out toward the teller. "Put all your money into this sack," he growled.

Trembling, the teller emptied his cash drawer.

"They ain't much there," Billy growled. "Get the rest out of the safe."

"I can't open the safe," the teller protested. "I don't know the combination."

"What the hell do you mean you don't know the combination? You work here, don't you?"

"Ye-yes," the teller stuttered. "But Mr. Edwards owns the bank. And he's the only one who knows the combination."

"All right, get him."

"He's out of town for the day," the teller replied. "He won't be back until late this evening."

Suddenly the front door opened and Terry, who didn't have the bottom half of his face masked, stuck his head in.

"Billy, Johnny, come on quick," he shouted. "Somebody seen these fellas with their hands up and went runnin' down the street for the sheriff. We got to get out of here!"

"Terry, you stupid sonofabitch!" Johnny shouted angrily. "You told 'em our names!"

"Open the goddamn safe!" Billy shouted, pointing his pistol toward the teller and cocking it.

The teller began to shake, uncontrollably. "Mister," he said. "Don't you think I would if I could? I don't want to die for someone else's money. I can't open that safe."

With a shout of frustrated rage, Billy brought his pistol down on the teller's head. With a groan, the teller dropped to the floor. Then, with the sack of money firmly clutched in his hand, Billy vaulted back over the teller's counter.

"Let's go!" he shouted.

As they reached the front door of the bank, someone from across the street fired at them with a heavy-gauge shotgun. The charge of double-aught buckshot missed the three robbers, but it did hit the front window, bringing it down with a loud crash.

Billy shot back and though he missed the man with the shotgun, he at least drove him back inside. The three bank robbers leaped into their saddles then started, at a gallop, down the street.

There had been several citizens out on the street and the sidewalks when the shooting erupted, and now they stood there watching in openmouthed shock as the three men who had just robbed their bank were getting away. Either none of them were armed, or else none of them wished to be a hero, for, other than the one attempt with a shotgun when the three men had first emerged from the bank, no one made any attempt to stop them.

At the end of the street a man stepped down off the boardwalk and out into the street. A flash of sunlight revealed the fact that a star was fastened to his vest.

"It's the sheriff!" Billy shouted. Billy shot at the sheriff, and the sheriff grabbed his shoulder, then staggered back a step. Billy shot a second time, as did Johnny and Terry and this time the sheriff went down under the fusillade of bullets.

By now the three men were out of town and pushing their horses hard to put as much distance between them and the town as they could.

"Is anyone comin' after us?" Billy shouted.

Terry, who was bringing up the rear, looked over his shoulder at the receding town. He saw no riders.

"No," he answered. "They ain't no one mounted. We got away clean!" He laughed out loud, whooping into the wind. "We got away clean!"

Sam Slater could tell by the way the outlaws were riding that they knew someone was on their trail. They didn't know who it was, or how many were after them, but they did know they were being dogged. They hadn't built a fire in the last three days, which meant that they, like Sam, were making do with cold jerky and tepid water.

Eating in the saddle didn't bother Sam. Having spent a while with the Apache, there were times when jerky and water would seem like a feast. He knew it was hard on the men he was trailing, though, because he had already found a couple of pieces of barely chewed jerky . . . spit out, no doubt, in anger over having to eat such fare.

The three outlaws who held up the bank in Sundown had gotten away with less than two hundred dollars because the teller had managed to convince them that the rest of the money was in the vault and he couldn't get to it. The robbery was bad enough, but on the way out of town they also killed Adam Prufrock, the deputy sheriff. Actually, the deputy hadn't really represented any particular threat to the three young robbers. Prufrock was an old man who had been given the job, almost as an act of charity. He didn't even carry a gun and served mostly as a cook for the few drunks and the occasional hell-raising cowhands who were the most frequent residents of the jail.

As a result of killing the old man, Billy Lobo, Terry Estes, and Johnny Singleton were now wanted for murder. The town of Sundown had offered a $250 reward for each of the men and the territorial government had added another

$250. That made the three men worth a total of fifteen hundred dollars . . . enough money to interest Sam Slater.

Sam was a bounty hunter. He wasn't just any bounty hunter—he was the most feared bounty hunter in the whole territory. Sometimes bounty hunters were also called regulators. There was, however, only one bounty hunter who was called The Regulator, and that was Sam Slater.

The trail led into a canyon. Sam didn't like this very much; there were too many opportunities for the outlaws to set up an ambush. He stopped for a moment and listened hard, trying to hear anything from ahead . . . the whicker of a horse, a voice, even the scratch of iron-shod hooves on stone. He could hear nothing.

Sam took a deep breath and pulled his rifle from the saddle sheath, then started into the canyon. He hadn't ridden more than a hundred yards into the canyon before all the hackles stood up on the back of his neck. He hadn't heard anything, nor had he seen anything. But, in that sixth sense developed by men who constantly live on the verge of instant death, he had felt something. He pulled his horse to a stop just as a bullet fried the air not six inches in front of his face. It hit a big rock on the other side of the trail, then whined off into space, while the canyon reverberated with the flat crack and high-pitched scream of the missed rifle shot. If he had not stopped at that very moment, he would have been killed.

With his rifle in his hand, Sam slid down, quickly. He slapped his horse to get him out of the line of fire, then ran toward a nearby line of large rocks, diving for cover just as another shot rang out. This one, like the first, was so close that he could hear the bullet passing.

"Who are you?" a voice called from a position partway up the canyon wall. "What are you doggin' us for?"

"The name's Slater," Sam called back. As soon as he shouted, he rolled to his right. This, too, was a fortunate move, for a bullet kicked up sand and pebble at the exact spot where he had been. Whoever was handling the long-gun up there was pretty good.

Sam moved to the end of the row of rocks and studied the canyon wall on the opposite side. There was no way he could get over there to them unseen, because he was on one side of the trail and they were on the other. He would have to cross an open space to start up the canyon wall and when he did that, he would be seen.

"You the one they call The Regulator?" Like the rifle shots before, the word "Regulator" echoed back and forth through the canyon.

"That's me," Sam shouted. Again, he rolled right after he called. This time, though, as he came out of the roll, he had the rifle to his shoulder, looking out across the barrel at the canyon wall toward the sound of the outlaw's voice. He saw the puff of smoke from the outlaw's rifle, then saw the outlaw raise up, slightly, to check on where his bullet had gone. It was a fatal move on the part of the outlaw, because for that one second, Sam had him in his sights. One second was all he needed. He squeezed the trigger; the Winchester roared and kicked back against his shoulder. A second later the outlaw tumbled down the wall on the other side of the canyon.

"Billy? Billy, are you hit?" a frightened voice called. Then, "Johnny! Johnny, I think he got Billy! What are we goin' to do?"

"There's still two of us agin the one of him," Johnny answered.

"But he's got us trapped up here!"

"Terry's right, Johnny," Sam called. "I do have you trapped up there."

"And we got you trapped down there," Johnny replied.

"Uh-uh," Sam said. "I've got my water and food with me. I'll just bet you fellas left yours with your horses."

"He's right, Johnny! We ain't got no water or nothin' up here."

"Shut up, Terry," Johnny called. "See if you can get a look at where he's at."

"I ain't movin' from here," Terry replied, fearfully.

"You yellow sonofabitch," Johnny snarled. "I'll take care of him. Then I'll take care of you."

Johnny began firing then. He wasn't as accurate as Billy had been, and that gave Sam a chance to improve his own position without fear of being hit. Crouching over, Sam ran behind the line of rocks, then darted across the little open gap so that he was on the same side of the trail as the two outlaws.

"Did you get him?" Terry called. From the sound of Terry's voice, Sam knew that he was no more than twenty yards away. He began looking around for a way up to him.

"I don't know," Johnny called. Johnny was a little farther into the canyon.

"You must'a got him. I don't see him or hear him movin' around down there."

Sam smiled. He realized then that they had managed to cross the trail unseen.

"Shoot again," Terry called.

"You shoot," Johnny replied. "I'll keep an eye open and if he returns your fire, I'll have him."

"The hell with that. I ain't makin' myself no decoy," Terry said.

"Shoot at him, you sonofabitch, or I'll shoot at you," Johnny growled.

Sam saw Terry raise up then. Unlike the others, who had rifles, Terry was armed only with a pistol. He began shooting, wildly. While Terry was shooting and looking anxiously toward the rocks where Sam had been, Sam managed to climb up a fissure until he was just a few feet away. He waited until the hammer on Terry's gun fell on an empty chamber.

"All right, I shot at him," Terry called. "Now I got to reload, it's your time."

"You dumb shit! You didn't do nothin' but waste your bullets," Johnny replied.

Terry turned around and slid back down to a seated position with his back against the rock, believing that, in that way, he was protected from Sam. He took a box of shells out of his shirt pocket, poured some into his hand, then began punching out the spent cartridges so he could push in the new. Sam waited until that moment, then leaped quickly across the gap, landing right in front of Terry.

"What the hell?" Terry shouted in surprise. That was as far as he got before Sam hit him with the butt of his rifle.

"Terry? Terry, what's goin' on over there? What'd you shout for?"

Sam stood up then, and looked toward the sound of Johnny's voice. It took him a few seconds, but he finally saw Johnny, squatted down behind a big rock. Like Terry, Johnny was protecting himself from someone he thought was on the opposite side of the trail. But, like Terry, he was totally exposed.

"Give it up, Johnny," Sam said, easily. "I've got a bead on you."

Surprised by the nearness of the challenging voice, Johnny looked around, then saw that Sam was right. There was nothing left for him to do but throw down his rifle. With a sigh, he did so.

"What's goin' to happen to us now?" he asked.

"I'm takin' the two of you in."

"To be hung?"

"Probably."

Johnny looked over to where Billy had been. "Did you kill Billy?"

"Yes."

Johnny sighed. "He's got the best of it, then."

CHAPTER 2

THAT SAME DAY, IN THE SMALL TOWN OF Salcedo, the normal afternoon's commerce was taking place when a rider came into town. He pulled up near the saloon, dismounted, and tied his horse to the hitchrail. He was rail-thin, with flat, gray eyes and several days' growth of beard. He took off his hat and rubbed a handkerchief across his face, then stuck the handkerchief back into his pocket. He glanced up and down the street as if making certain that there was no potential threat, then pushed his way through the swinging batwing doors.

He was wearing a gun strapped low on his right hip, and once inside, he stepped away from the door so that he wasn't backlighted, then paused for a moment before he moved on. Only when his eyes were fully adjusted to the dimmer light did he walk over to the bar.

"You know who that is?" one of the saloon's patrons whispered to his table partner.

"Can't say as I do."

"That there is Rufus Colby. I reckon you've heard of him, ain't you?"

"Yeah, I've heard of him. He's a . . ."

"He's a gunfighter," the first one interrupted, as though he didn't want to be cheated out of imparting the information.

"He's supposed to be . . ."

"Really fast," the first one said.

"What do you reckon he's doin' here?"

"I don't know. Look at that gun handle. You think there's any notches on it?"

"I don't know, and I don't aim to look none too close."

Colby, unaware that he was the subject of a whispered conversation—or perhaps aware, but unconcerned—stepped up to the bar and slapped a coin down.

"Whiskey," he grunted.

"I'll be glad to serve you some whiskey, Mr. Colby. Only we ain't got no blended whiskey left. That cowboy down there just bought our last bottle. Our trade liquor ain't that bad though."

Colby turned to look at the cowboy. "I'd like to buy the whiskey from you," he said.

The cowboy shook his head. "Mister, I been eatin' trail dust for two weeks thinkin' about comin' in here for a good bottle of whiskey. I aim to keep it for myself."

"I'll pay double."

"That's mighty generous of you, but, thank you, no. I plan to keep it."

Colby put some money on the bar and slid it toward the cowboy.

"Mister, don't you hear good?" the cowboy asked. "I told you, I ain't sellin' my whiskey."

"Either pick up the money, or go for your gun," Colby said.

"What?"

"I said, pull your gun or give me the bottle."

"You're aimin' to throw down on me over a bottle of whiskey?"

"Give him the bottle, boy," the bartender said. "Don't you know who this is?"

"I don't know, and I don't care," the cowboy said. "I don't plan to oblige 'im with a gunfight or the bottle."

Colby pulled his gun and fired. Pink mist sprayed from the cowboy's earlobe and he slapped his hand up to the side of his head with a howl of pain. By the time the smoke cleared, the pistol was back in Colby's holster.

"Give me the bottle," Colby ordered.

With his left hand still pressed against his ear, the cowboy shoved the bottle down the bar with his right. "Here," he said. "Take the goddamn bottle." He reached for the money.

"Leave it," Colby said. "You didn't take it when I offered it to you."

The cowboy stared at Colby through hate-filled eyes, then, still keeping his hand pressed against the side of his head, rushed out of the saloon. Colby poured himself a drink, then turned back to the bar, studying, carefully, the mirror behind the bar.

"He didn't mean nothin' by challengin' you like that, Mr. Colby," the bartender said. "He's just a boy, that's all."

"You know of a town name of Puxico?" Colby asked as he raised the glass to his lips.

"Sure do. It's 'bout ten, maybe fifteen miles north of here," the bartender said. "It's a mining town. You goin' there?"

Colby tossed the liquor down, then slid the glass across the bar to indicate that he wanted another.

"A friend of mine is the sheriff over there. I hear tell he is putting on deputies. Thought I might join him."

"You mean you're goin' to be a deputy?" the bartender asked in surprise. "I never would've thought you would be a . . ." Suddenly the bartender realized that he might be overstepping his bounds, so he swallowed the last of his sentence. "'Course," he added, "I'm sure you would make a fine deputy."

Someone got up from one of the tables then, and walked over to the end of the bar. He had red hair and a red beard, and Colby saw that he had been studying him fairly intently from the moment he had entered the saloon.

"Hey, you, Colby," he finally said.

Colby looked toward him, but he didn't speak.

"That is your name, ain't it? Ain't you Rufus Colby?"

"If you're a bounty hunter, mister, there's no paper out on me," Colby said.

"I ain't no bounty hunter."

"You got somethin' stickin' in your craw, mister. What is it?" Colby asked.

"The name is Martin. My brother was Gene Martin. Does that name mean anything to you?"

"Can't say as it does," Colby replied.

"He was a deputy sheriff up in Rodsburg. It still doesn't mean anything to you?"

Colby turned away from the bar so that he was facing Martin.

"I had a little scrape up in Rodsburg once," he said.

"A little scrape, you call it? Mister, I don't call killin' a little scrape," Martin said.

"I guess that all depends on who's gettin' killed," Colby said.

"It was my brother who got killed," Martin said.

"Yeah, well, like I said, it was a little scrape. Better him than me."

"I've chased you to hell and back, you sonofabitch!" Martin shouted.

At the sound of Martin's words of challenge, everyone in the saloon began making haste to move out of the way. Tables scraped against the floor and chairs turned over as the men hurried out of any potential line of fire.

"You found me. What do you aim to do now?"

Martin stepped away from the bar and held his hands out to either side.

"As you can see, I'm not armed," he said. He doubled up his fists. "But I don't need a gun to take the likes of you."

As Martin started toward Colby, Colby pulled his pistol and shot Martin in the right knee. The impact of the bullet knocked Martin down.

"Stay down there, and you might live." Colby said.

Using the bar to assist him, Martin got back onto his feet. The wound in his right knee was bleeding profusely and the bottom of his trouser leg was already soaked in blood.

Colby shot him again, putting a ball in his left knee. When Martin went down this time, he was unable to get up.

"Give me a gun," Martin said to the bartender. His voice was racked with pain.

"Martin, let it go," the bartender said.

"I said give me a gun, goddamnit!" Martin repeated, louder and with more insistence.

"Give him a gun," Colby said, quietly.

"You don't want to . . ."

"Give him a gun," Colby said again. He neither raised his voice nor changed the inflection, but said the words as flatly and unemotionally as if he had just inquired of the time.

With a sigh, the bartender pulled a pistol from behind the bar, then leaned over to hand it down to Martin.

"Put the gun on the floor in front of you," Colby ordered.

"I should've shot you in the first place, you bastard," Martin growled as he lay the gun on the floor.

Colby smiled, a small, evil smile. "Whenever you feel lucky," he said.

Martin took a deep breath, then made a desperate grab for the gun. Colby watched him, and waited until Martin had the gun in his hand and was raising it from the floor before he even began his own draw. Seeing this, Martin had a momentary belief that he was going to win. Then, as he was still bringing his pistol up, Colby drew and fired. His bullet caught Martin in the chest and pitched him back onto the floor. His arms flopped uselessy beside him and the unfired gun fell into a half-full spittoon.

Colby looked at his victim for a moment, then put the pistol back in his holster. He reached for the bottle of whiskey.

"Can't say as I got a very warm reception here," he said to the bartender. "Think I'll mosey on up to Puxico, where I've got friends. I figure I'll be a bit more welcome there."

Colby walked through the door, while behind him a cloud of gunsmoke drifted slowly toward the ceiling and a man lay dead on the barroom floor. Once outside, without so much as a glance back into the saloon, Colby mounted his horse and rode away. The bottle of blended whiskey glinted once in the sun.

Puxico began as a mining town. For more than two years the Consolidated Mining Company had taken as much silver out of the Puxico digs as had been mined at any other place in the country. Now, though most of the silver veins were played out, there was still a large amount of copper remaining. This allowed the more settled hard-rock miners to make a living, though the work was harder and the payoff less.

During Puxico's heyday there had been more than one way to mine silver. Some did it with a pick and shovel, others did it with cards, or liquor, or a pretty smile and a well-shaped thigh.

Not everyone was upset with the playout of the silver mines. Silver, like gold, attracted get-rich-quick people. Copper, on the other hand, tended to attract only the most industrious of the miners . . . the mining engineers and the hardworking men who went down into the shafts. These were the steady, sober-minded men who wanted to start families and build a town. That also tended to attract stores, banks, schools, doctors, and freight and stage lines. There were also a few ranches nearby to take advantage of the railroad. That was what the citizens of Puxico wanted, and that was what was happening, until a man named Charlie Jessup had other ideas.

Charlie Jessup was a short, unattractive man with a pockmarked face, a drooping black beard, a hawklike nose, and narrow, obsidian eyes. It was, perhaps, that unattractiveness which made him an outcast from society. As a result, he had developed absolutely no social skills. He did, however, have one skill which marked him as a man with whom others would have to reckon. Charlie Jessup was a deadly shot, snake-fast on the draw, and with so few moral compunctions about killing that he could take the life of another as easily as he could step on a cockroach.

Jessup had come to Puxico when the mines were still producing silver. He had been hired by the mining company to provide security for the silver shipments. Some, who knew of Jessup's spotted past—he had robbed a few banks and held up a stage or two—suggested that using him to guard the silver was like setting the fox to watch the hen coop. Others insisted that you must "set a thief to catch a thief" and saw no problem whatever with using Jessup to guard the shipments.

After the silver played out, however, there was no longer a need to provide guards over the ore shipments. That was because it took so much copper to turn a profit that the freight wagon gave way to the railroad as the prime carrier. Thus, by the time Consolidated Mining completed its changeover from silver to copper, Jessup and his men found themselves out of work.

Those who breathed a sigh of relief over that fact soon learned, to their dismay, that Jessup had no intention of leaving Puxico. Instead, he bullied a few of the town's officials into appointing him as the town sheriff, and his men as deputies. Now, with badges on their vests, the Jessup gang had free run of the entire town.

His reign of terror began with the saloon, where he extracted a "tax" from each drink, supposedly to pay for his protection. That quickly extended to the other businesses in town as well—hotels, restaurants, stores, even the livery stable.

In addition to the tax Jessup and his deputies collected, they enjoyed the privilege of a "special reduced rate" for the goods they bought from any of the town's merchants. What they paid was so little that it was practically stealing. Always bullies, they moved along the boardwalks, or through the streets of the town, pushing any and all out of their way. They would sometimes go so far as to pistol-whip some poor soul who was too slow in avoiding them. There had even been a few killings, usually over a dispute in a card game, but always justified as "self-defense" or "killed while resisting arrest for card cheating."

The situation eventually reached the point where very few of the decent citizens of Puxico would dare venture out of their homes. That hurt the business of the town's merchants, and as the legitimate stores began closing, the town began dying.

As Puxico began dying, however, it flared brightly, for drinking, gambling, and whoring became its major industries. News of the "wide-open" town spread throughout the territory, and it began to attract new residents. The new residents, however, were not the kind of people the original citizens of the town wanted, for they were nothing more than carbon copies of Jessup and his men. As more hoodlums arrived, the number of those who were sucking out the life's blood of the town became disproportionate to the number of those whose industriousness supplied the life's blood of the town. Like an animal being drained by leeches, the town was slowly, but inexorably, sinking to its knees.

This was the condition of things when Rufus arrived in Puxico. It took him only a few minutes to find Charlie Jessup and offer his services.

"Rufus, you old saddle tramp, you," Jessup greeted him warmly. "How long has it been? A year? Two years?"

"Nearly three," Colby said. "Back in Dodge, I think."

"Yeah, Dodge City," Jessup said. He smiled. "It was a wide-open town then. Like Puxico is now. So, you want to be a part of it, do you?"

"If you got room for me," Colby replied.

"Hell, I always got room for a good man," Jessup said. "Outside of Muley Zorn, I don't have anyone around me who's worth a pitcher of piss."

"Why do you keep 'em around, then?"

"The more deputies I have, the more scared the locals are," Jessup explained. "And the more scared they are, the easier it is to keep things under control."

"Are the pickin's good enough to go around?"

"If you know where to pick," Jessup replied with a smile. "Tell you what. If you want to stay on and help me run things around here, I'll make you my second deputy."

"Your second deputy?"

"Muley is my first."

"Don't think I've ever heard of this Muley."

"He's a big sonofabitch," Jessup said. "Half man and half bear. He's good to have around. He can keep more people straight with his fists than I can with a gun . . . and without havin' to kill anyone."

"It don't bother me to kill anyone," Colby said.

Jessup laughed. "Hell, me neither, when it needs doin'. But we're the law in Puxico, and we got to think that way. We can't just go round killin' the citizens 'cause we feel like it."

"What do I get as your second deputy?"

"Me, you, and Muley split the business tax," Jessup said. "That's where the real money is. The others have to collect a personal tax. The personal tax is pretty slim pickin's, and it's gettin' slimmer. Now, what do you say? Are you in?"

Colby smiled. "Yeah, sure, why not?" he asked. "It might be fun, bein' a deputy."

CHAPTER 3

TO THE THREE COWBOYS APPROACHING Puxico after dark that evening, there was little sign that the town was dying. The bright glow of lights from the busy saloons were visible from far out in the desert, and, as they drew even closer to the town, they could hear the sounds of reverie: loud voices, the high-pitched trill of a woman's laughter, and the tinkling of pianos.

"They's three things I want when I get to town," one of the cowboys said. Though his real name was Edgar Morris, he was known to everyone as Poke. "I want me a steak, a bottle of whiskey, and a woman."

"You got them three things just backwards, Poke," Willie said. "I aim to get me a woman, a bottle of whiskey, and then a steak."

Josh laughed at the other two. "Why you fellas want to take the time to mess with a steak and a bottle of whiskey beats me," he said.

"You mean you aim to just get a woman?" Poke asked.

"That ain't what I mean a'tall," Josh said. "I want three things, just like you two boys."

"And what would them three things be?" Willie wanted to know.

"A woman, another woman, and another woman," Josh said, and all three men laughed.

Like moths drawn to a flame, the three cowboys stopped in front of the Silver Strike Saloon. The Silver Strike had been built during Puxico's heyday of silver mining, and it had a real mahogany bar, a gilt-edged mirror, and an ample supply of a decent grade of whiskey. There were several large jars of pickled eggs and sausages on the bar, and a fresh-daily supply of towels tied to rings every few feet on the customers' side of the bar to provide the drinkers with a means of wiping their hands. The walls were decorated with game-heads and pictures. The obligatory reclining nude was behind the bar, while on the opposite wall was a mountain scene, a cool, snow-covered pine forest beneath a silver moon and a starry vault of night sky. In the latter picture a train, with its huge headlight stabbing forward, was crossing a high, wooden trestle. Every window of every car in the train was unrealistically and brightly lighted, and every window had a smiling passenger's face.

All of this had been put in place by Parmeter, the saloon's owner and bartender, before Jessup and his bunch had taken over the town. That had given the saloon a bit of respectability, though the effort seemed a mockery, now that Jessup was in charge of things.

The upstairs area didn't extend all the way to the front of the building, so the main room of the saloon was big, with exposed rafters just below the high-peaked ceiling. There were at least a dozen tables in the large, common room, and they were arranged around a couple of potbellied stoves. The stoves weren't in use now because it was the middle of August. There was, however, a lingering tang of woodsmoke near the stoves, evidence of their use during the winter season.

When the three cowboys pushed through the batwing doors, they were met almost immediately by one of the girls who worked at the saloon.

"Hello, boys," she said with a practiced smile. "My name is Suzie. Welcome to the Silver Strike."

"Well, boys, I got me a girl," Poke said, putting his arm around her. "Ain't that right, Suzie?" He looked at the others. "What are you two goin' to do?"

"Oh, I'm not just your girl, honey. I'm everyone's girl. You ask anyone, they'll tell you. Suzie is everyone's girl."

"For sure?" Poke asked. He laughed. "All right, Suzie, if you want to be everyone's girl, that's jake with me. Come on and have a drink with us."

Suzie laughed. "That's just what I'm planning to do."

What Suzie didn't tell the boys, and what they didn't know, was that she had just left one of the other tables a moment earlier, after having had a disagreement with one of the men. The person with whom she had had the disagreement was Roy Kilgore, who also happened to be one of Charlie Jessup's deputies. The disagreement was over whether or not Suzie would go upstairs with Kilgore. It wasn't over whether or not Suzie was that kind of a girl . . . she *was* that kind of a girl. It wasn't over money, either, for Kilgore was more than willing to meet Suzie's price. But Suzie felt that, whore or not, she should be able to say who she would take for a customer and who she wouldn't. Kilgore was a brutal man who enjoyed hitting women, and Suzie wanted no part of that. Now, as Suzie escorted the three young cowboys to an empty table, she was followed by Kilgore's angry, staring eyes.

Within half an hour the three young cowboys were well on their way to getting drunk from cheap whiskey. Then, after some bragging about his prowess as a dancer, Poke decided to demonstrate. He got up and began dancing around the table. When his spurs got tangled up, he fell flat on his back. Suzie and the other two cowboys laughed heartily, then Willie got up.

"You call that dancin'? You can't dance worth a damn," he said. "Look at me, Suzie. Let me show you how it's really done."

Willie threw his hat onto the floor, then began dancing around it. But, like Poke before him, he tripped. Unlike Poke, however, he didn't fall on the floor. Instead, he fell against one of the other tables. That just happened to be the table where Kilgore was sitting.

"Get away from me, you drunken bastard," Kilgore growled, shoving him roughly.

Josh, who was the oldest and least drunk of the three cowboys, saw the badge pinned to Kilgore's shirt. He saw also that Willie was about to react to being shoved, so he jumped in, quickly, and apologized.

"My friend didn't mean nothin', Deputy," he said. "We been workin' hard all week and are just tryin' to have a good time, that's all."

"Yeah? Well, if he winds up on me again, I'll end his fun . . . permanent."

The bartender came around from behind the bar then to speak to the deputy.

"Don't be so hard on those boys, Kilgore. They're just workin' cowboys who don't mean no harm," he said. "I've seen 'em in here before."

Kilgore pointed to the bar. "Parmeter, you just get on back behind the bar there, where you belong," he growled. "This here ain't none of your concern."

"I own the saloon," Parmeter said. "If it ain't my concern, whose concern is it?"

Kilgore pointed to his badge. "I'd say this here comes under the headin' of keepin' the peace," he said. "Now, you go on about your business an' I'll go about mine."

Parmeter started to say something else, then thought the better of it. He was as much subject to the whims of the sheriff and his deputies as any other merchant in town, and as resentful of it. With a sigh, he returned to the bar as Kilgore had ordered.

During the altercation the piano player had stopped playing, and for a moment there was a dead silence as everyone looked on with interest to see what was about to happen.

"Piano player, play," Poke shouted. "How'n hell can I dance if you don't play?"

"Poke," Josh said. "Poke, maybe you've had enough dancin' for one evenin'."

"Like hell I have," Poke replied. "I come to town to have a good time an' that's what I'm goin' to have. I ain't seen nothin' but the backside of cows for more'n a week now, an' I aim to let off a little steam. Play some music."

The piano player looked over at Parmeter, who, with a slight nod of his head, indicated that the music could continue. With that, the piano player turned back toward his instrument and put his fingers on the keyboard. A second later the saloon was once again filled with the raucous melody of "Buffalo Gals."

The music seemed to ease the tension, for the laughter and conversation resumed as easily as if it had never been interrupted in the first place.

With the situation under control, Josh left Suzie and his two friends and, after a few words of conversation with one of the other girls, went upstairs with her.

"Hey, Poke, do you see where Josh's gone?" Willie asked a few moments later.

"No, where'd he go?" Poke asked.

"He took him a woman upstairs. I'm goin' to get me one too. You just goin' to dance all night, or what?"

"Yeah, but I ain't goin' to dance by myself," Poke answered. "Come on, Suzie, dance with me," he called, waving his arms to invite Suzie to join him.

Laughing at Poke's antics, Suzie stood up.

"I'd be glad to join you, Cowboy," she said. She joined him on the floor, hooked her arm through his, and began to dance.

There were three other men at the table with Kilgore. Like Kilgore, they were wearing deputies' badges. One of them laughed, then pointed at Poke.

"Hell, I know now why you couldn't get ole Suzie to go upstairs with you, Kilgore. You didn't dance none with her. Looks to me like that cowboy has got your girl," he suggested.

"Yeah? Well, I'd like to see how long he's plannin' on keepin' her," Kilgore answered, unamused by the joke. He got up and started toward the bar. Instead of going directly to the bar, however, his circuitous route took him by where Poke and Suzie were dancing. They didn't notice him approaching, for by now they were oblivious to everything around them except the music, each other, and the fun they were having.

As Kilgore passed by, he stuck his leg out, then pushed Poke down.

"Hey, mister, what the hell you think you're doin'?" Poke asked, angrily.

"Cowboy, you're so drunk you can't even stand up," Kilgore said. "I guess maybe you'd better spend the night in jail. Come on, you're comin' with me."

"Like hell I am," Poke said, reaching awkwardly for his gun.

"Watch 'im, Kilgore! He's goin' for his gun!" one of the other deputies shouted, though the warning wasn't necessary, for Kilgore was already starting his own draw.

With Poke lying on the floor and Kilgore standing, the advantage was all Kilgore's as the two men drew their pistols. Kilgore fired from point-blank range, putting a bullet in Poke's heart before Poke could even clear his holster.

In the meantime, Willie, who had walked over to the bar to find his own girl, turned back around just in time to see Kilgore shooting Poke.

"No!" Willie shouted, pulling his own pistol. He shot Kilgore, then was himself cut down by Rufus Colby, who, sitting at a table in the back of the room with Muley Zorn, had just joined the fray.

After the explosions of gunfire, an eerie silence fell over the saloon as the other patrons stood there looking at the three dead bodies, dumbstruck by the suddenness of events. A heavy cloud of blue-black smoke from the three discharges began drifting up toward the top of the room. There was a scampering of feet on the upper-floor landing as the men and women who had been engaged in the private rooms now scampered to the head of the stairs for a look down into the common room to see what had happened.

One of those on the upper landing was Josh. When he peered over the railing he saw his two friends lying in their own pools of blood. "Poke! Willie!" he shouted, starting down the stairs toward them.

"That there's the other one!" one of the deputies who had been sitting at the table with Kilgore said.

Rufus raised his pistol.

"You don't need to shoot," Muley said, crossing the room in a few quick, long strides. He reached out to grab Josh.

Josh had no idea that he was in danger. As a result he made no effort to get away, which meant that Muley had no difficulty in aprehending him.

"Hey!" he shouted. "What are you doing? Let me go! Those are my pals lyin' there. That's Poke, and Willie! Let me go! I've got to see them!"

"Mister, you don't got to do nothin' but go to jail," Muley growled. Muley was such a big and powerfully built man that he was able to control Josh all by himself.

CHAPTER 4

**The town of Sundown,
fifteen miles east of Puxico**

THERE WAS NO BUILDING SPECIFICALLY designated as a courthouse in Sundown. As a result of this deficiency, Judge Jeremiah Townsdale, the visiting circuit judge, had to hold his court in the schoolhouse. That caused no difficulty, as the school was vacant for the summer.

Sheriff Daniel Barkett stepped to the front of the improvised courtroom, then looked out over the gallery. The place was filled to overflowing with people who had come to see the trial of the two men Sam Slater had brought in. Barkett wasn't surprised by that. Feelings were running high, because the deputy killed by the bank robbers during their escape was one of the town's most beloved citizens. There was also some interest in the fact that this was a capital trial, the first ever to be held in Sundown. The fact that the desperadoes had been brought in by none other than The Regulator himself added a degree of excitement to the situation.

"All rise!" Sheriff Barkett said.

There was a scrape of chairs and a rustle of pants, petticoats, and skirts as the spectators in the makeshift courtroom stood. A spittoon rang as one male member of the gallery made a last-second, accurate expectoration of his tobacco quid.

"Oyez, oyez, oyez, this circut court, meeting in Sundown, is now in session, the Honorable Judge Jeremiah Townsdale presiding."

Judge Townsdale took his seat in front of the assembly, then looked out over the court through clear, piercing blue eyes.

"Be seated."

The gallery sat, then watched as the two prisoners were brought into the room for the trial.

"Terry Estes and Johnny Singleton, you are charged with bank robbery and murder," Judge Townsdale said. "Are you represented by counsel?"

"They are, Your Honor," a man said, standing to address the court.

"And who are you?"

"I am Fenton Smith, Your Honor, duly authorized by the bar to practice law in this territory."

"And you have been appointed by the court to defend these men?"

"Yes, Your Honor."

"And how do they plead?"

"To the charge of bank robbery, guilty, Your Honor. To the charge of murder, not guilty."

"Very well, let the trial proceed," Judge Townsdale said.

The case for the prosecution was quick and simple. There were three witnesses in the bank during the time of the robbery, all of whom identified the two defendants as having been two of the three men who committed the robbery. There were even more witnesses, nine in fact, who identified them as two of the three men who witnessed the shooting of Deputy Prufrock. The doctor testified that he took four bullets from the deputy's body, two of which were .44-caliber and two of which were .31-caliber rounds. Billy Lobo was the only one who had been armed with a .44. Both Estes and Singleton had been carrying .31-caliber pistols.

At the conclusion of the doctor's testimony, Fenton Smith stood up for cross-examination.

"Doctor Porter, of the four bullets you took from the deputy's body, can you determine which one killed him?"

"There were two which would have been fatal," the doctor said. "Not knowing the order in which they were fired, I couldn't determine which one actually killed the deputy."

"What was the caliber of the two bullets?"

"One was a .44, the other was a .31 caliber."

"I see. That means then, does it not, that the other two bullets would not have proven fatal?"

"There's no way to actually determine that," Dr. Porter said. "Infectious gangrene could have caused either of the other bullets to be fatal."

"But, arriving on the scene as quickly as you did, do you not feel that you would have been able to save the deputy, if it had not been for the two fatal bullets?"

"Yes, I think I could have."

"Doctor, both Mr. Estes and Mr. Singleton were armed with .31-caliber pistols. Which of their pistols fired the fatal shot?"

"Well, I . . . I don't know," the doctor said. "There's no way of telling that."

"In fact, there is, Doctor. There is a new technique, recently developed as a result of police investigation procedures in the East, by which it can be determined which gun fires which bullet."

"Perhaps so, but we have no such ability here," the doctor replied.

"Then you cannot say which of my two clients fired the fatal shot?"

"No, I cannot."

"Thank you, Doctor."

Later, during his summation to the jury, Fenton Smith made much of the fact that no one could tell, with certainty, which of his two clients actually fired the fatal bullet.

"One of my clients is guilty of murder," he told

the jury. "The other is guilty of bank robbery, but he is not guilty of murder. Which one is it? That is something we may never know, gentlemen, and, because the law requires that guilt can only be established if a jury is convinced, beyond reasonable doubt, then we may never know who fired the fatal bullet.

"That leaves us with a dilemma, gentlemen, for we cannot hang an innocent man. Our justice system is designed to protect the innocent. It is better to let the guilty man live . . . than to put to death an innocent man.

"Also, let us not forget that there was a third party involved in this business, and he was using a .44-caliber pistol. He was the only one using a .44-caliber pistol, and, as we know from Dr. Porter's testimony, one of the .44-caliber bullets could have been the fatal shot. That man, Billy Lobo, has already paid the supreme penalty for his action, since he was killed in the process of his apprehension.

"That means, then, that Deputy Prufrock has been avenged. However, we are an enlightened race and we know that it is not the purpose of the court to exact vengeance. . . . It is the purpose of the court to seek justice. But there can be no justice if an innocent man is hanged. And since we do not know which of these two men fired the bullet which could have been fatal, we cannot determine with any certainty which one of them should be hanged. Therefore, the spirit of true justice, gentlemen of the jury, demands that we spare them both. My clients admit their guilt to the charge of bank robbery. Find them guilty of that, and assess the penalty such a crime demands. But, in the name of humanity, enlightenment, and yes, justice, I ask that you return a verdict of 'not guilty' to the charge of murder."

Fenton Smith's closing argument was most impassioned, but the prosector was also a man of persuasive logic.

"It doesn't matter which one fired the fatal bullet," he told the jury. "Both of these men fired at Deputy Prufrock with the intent to kill. The learned and capable counsel for the defense is suggesting that because one of these two men is less proficient in the use of a firearm than the other, then he should be found not guilty of murder. But I would remind the jury that any unlawful death which might occur during the commission of a felony is to be considered murder in the first degree, said guilt to fall equally upon all perpetrators. Armed bank robbery, gentlemen, is a felony, which means the unlawful death of Deputy Prufrock is murder in the first degree . . . to be shared equally by all perpetrators. Both Estes and Singleton have admitted to the crime of bank robbery; therefore, they stand condemned by their own words."

The jury retired to the cloakroom to decide the case. They returned fifteen minutes later with a verdict of guilty on both counts, for both defendants.

Judge Townsdale heard the verdict, then cleared his throat and looked over at the sheriff.

"Sheriff Barkett, would you position the prisoners before the bench for sentencing, please?"

"Yes, Your Honor."

The two men were brought before the bench, where they stood with their heads bowed contritely.

"Mr. Estes and Mr. Singleton, as I am sure you would both testify, you have had a fair and honest hearing. In fact, I would like to publicly compliment your attorney, Mr. Smith, for what I thought was a very good defense. Nevertheless, the jury, having heard all the testimony and all the arguments from both sides, has found you guilty. Therefore it is my unpleasant duty to sentence both of you to be hanged by the neck until you are dead. This sentence will be carried out at two o'clock in the afternoon, one week from today."

CHAPTER 5

Puxico

"HEY YOU, PRISONER, WAKE UP," MULEY called.

Josh opened his eyes and saw that he was lying in a jail cell. At first he didn't understand how he got there, then he realized that he had gotten very drunk the night before.

"Ohh," he groaned, putting his hand to his head as he sat up on the bunk. "Was I that drunk?" He looked around the cell. "Where's Poke and Willie?"

"They're pushin' up daisies by now."

"Pushin' up daisies?" he asked in confusion. "What do you mean?"

"I mean they're deader'n shit," Muley said, laughing.

It wasn't until that moment that Josh remembered the scene from the night before of his two friends lying in pools of blood on the barroom floor. He jumped up quickly and ran to the door of his cell, wrapping his fingers around the steel bars.

"I've got to get out of here!" he shouted. "I've got to get back to the ranch and tell Mr. Howard."

Muley was a very large man, and Josh remembered now that this was the one who'd brought him to jail last night.

"Muley," Josh said. "Your name is Muley, ain't it?"

"Not to you, it ain't," Muley replied. "To you, it's Deputy Zorn."

"Deputy Zorn, I have to get out of here. How much is my fine? When can I pay it?"

Muley laughed. "Fine? That's funny, mister. That's 'bout the funniest thing I ever heard. I ain't never heard of no one payin' a fine for murder."

"Murder? What are you talkin' about? I didn't murder anyone."

"You are in here for murder, boy. You, and them other two galoots that was with you, killed Deputy Kilgore last night."

"Why, I . . . I did no such thing," Josh said. "I was upstairs with a whore when all that happened. If you'll let me go over to the saloon I'll find her an' she'll tell you."

"You ain't goin' nowhere," Muley said. "You're goin' to have your trial right here, soon as the sheriff comes in."

"The sheriff? What about the judge?"

"Don't you know, boy? In Puxico, Sheriff Jessup is the judge."

Groaning, Josh walked back over to his bunk and sat down, holding his head in his hands. He was still in that position a few minutes later when he heard Muley speak again.

"Stand up, boy," Muley said. "Your trial's about to begin."

"Where?"

"Right here, in the jailhouse," Muley said. "It saves lots of time."

"This ain't no courtroom," Josh said. "And this ain't no trial."

"If I say it's a trial, it's a trial," a new voice said. The speaker had a pockmarked face and a droopy, black mustache. He pulled up a chair and set down.

"You're Sheriff Jessup, ain't you?" Josh asked.

"I'm Sheriff Jessup when I'm sheriffin'," Jessup answered. "I'm Judge Jessup when I'm judgin'. These here men, who are my deputies, are goin' to act as the jury."

Josh looked toward the front of his cell and saw that, in addition to Muley, there were six men. All were wearing badges.

"Deputies can't be the jury, can they?" Josh asked.

"They can in my court."

"They's only six of 'em."

"That's all we need in my court. Now, you're

charged with the murder of Deputy Roy Kilgore. How do you plead?"

"I didn't kill nobody!" Josh insisted.

"Maybe you didn't, but you come into town with them two boys and that makes you guilty of aidin' and abettin' a murder."

"Wait a minute! Don't I get a lawyer?"

"You got enough money for a lawyer?"

"Yes. I've got ten dollars here in my—" Josh began feeling around in his pockets, and soon realized that he had no money at all. "My money," he said. "It's gone. Someone took my money."

"Then you can't afford a lawyer," Jessup replied. "Which means the court'll have to appoint one for you. Muley, you are his lawyer."

"All right, Judge," Muley said, smiling broadly.

"Now, how do you plead?"

"I plead not guilty," Josh said.

Jessup held up his hand. "You've got a lawyer now, boy. He'll plead for you. Counselor, how do you plead your client?"

"I plead him guilty, Your Honor," Muley said without consulting with Josh.

Jessup turned toward the six "jurors" and said, "You've heard the counselor for the defendant plead this here prisoner guilty. How do you find?"

"We find the sonofabitch guilty, Judge," one of the jurors said.

Using his pistol as a gavel, Jessup brought it down sharply on the table. "Boy, this court finds you guilty, and sentences you to hang. Get him out there to the tree, boys, and let's get this over with," he said.

"Wait a minute!" Josh said. "You mean you're takin' me out to hang right now? I don't get no chance to appeal to a higher court?"

Jessup and the others laughed.

"Boy, there ain't no higher court in Puxico," Muley said.

When Mrs. Pruitt went into the Miller General Mercantile Store that morning, she knew nothing of what had taken place in the Silver Strike Saloon the night before, or of the "trial" that had just been conducted down in the sheriff's office a few minutes earlier. She knew only that Lem Miller was expecting a new shipment of yarn and she wanted to see if it had arrived.

"Mama, would you buy me a stick of hoarhound candy?" her seven-year-old son, Jimmy, asked.

"No," Mrs. Pruitt said. "It will spoil your lunch. You just be a good boy and stay out of things while I look around."

Disappointed, Jimmy walked over to look through the front window of the store.

"Good morning, Mrs. Pruitt," Lem Miller said, smiling broadly. "I'll just bet you are here to check on that yarn, aren't you?"

"Yes, did it come in?"

"It did, I'm happy to say. It arrived on yesterday's train. Why don't you let Mrs. Miller show it to you."

"Thank you."

"Mama," Jimmy called.

"Not now, Jimmy."

"Mama, there are a bunch of men out there around that big tree."

"Not now, Jimmy. Can't you see I'm busy?"

Mrs. Pruitt was too interested in looking at the skeins of colorful yarn to pay any attention to Jimmy, but Lem Miller looked up when Jimmy mentioned several men around a tree. Curious as to what might be going on, he walked over to look through the window.

"Oh, my God," he said.

"What is it, Lem?"

"That's Sheriff Jessup and his deputies. They're fixin' to hang someone."

"Jimmy!" Mrs. Pruitt said. "Jimmy, you get away from that window!"

"I want to watch, Mama," Jimmy replied.

"You get away from that window right now, you hear me?" Mrs. Pruitt ordered, coming over to grab her son by the shoulder.

"Lem," Mrs. Miller said. "Lem, can't you do something?"

Miller looked at his wife with a helpless expression on his face. "What do you propose that I do, woman?" he asked. "Go out there and single-handedly stop them?"

"Yes. No. I mean, I don't know. But we can't just stand by and let this happen, can we?"

"I'll . . . I'll go out and see if I can find out what's goin' on," Miller said.

When Miller stepped out onto the boardwalk in front of his store, he saw Jarred Appleby and Doc Sweeny standing there, watching the proceedings. Their faces were contorted in horror and impotent rage.

"Appleby, what is this?" Miller asked, pointing toward the tree. "What's goin' on over there?"

"Didn't you hear the gunshots down at the saloon last night?" Appleby asked.

"I suppose I did," Miller said. "But there are gunshots pert' near every night. I didn't pay no mind to 'em."

"These gunshots were different," Appleby said. "Kilgore got himself killed."

"Kilgore?" Miller looked around before he spoke again. "Well, I can't say that he's any great loss." He looked over at a young man who was standing alongside a buckboard, his arms tied to his side. "Is that the one who killed him?"

"No. The one who killed him is dead."

"Well, who's this, then?"

"His name is Josh Speedwell," Doc Sweeny said. "He's a cowboy from the Bar-H spread. He and two of his friends came in for a little fun last night. Things got out of hand. . . . There was a shootout, Kilgore and the other two cowboys are dead, and they're about to hang this boy."

"You mean they're goin' to lynch him? No trial or anything?"

"Oh, he had a trial all right," Appleby said. "If you can call it that. Sheriff Jessup held it down in the jail this mornin'."

"Jessup is the sheriff, not the judge."

"You want to go tell him that?" Appleby asked.

Miller didn't answer, though the expression on his face showed that he had no desire to confront Charlie Jessup.

"The boy would've been better off if he had been killed in the shootout along with his two friends," Miller said.

"He wasn't in the shootout," Appleby said.

"What do you mean he wasn't in the shootout? I thought you said he was with the other two," Miller said.

"He rode into town with them," Appleby said. "But from what I hear, he was upstairs with one of Parmeter's whores when all the shootin' started."

"He was? You mean he didn't have anything to do with the shootin' at all?"

"Nope."

"Oh, my God! Then this is nothing but murder," Miller said.

"That's exactly what it is," Doc Sweeny agreed. "We are about to witness a murder."

The three men watched, helplessly, as the young cowboy was helped up onto the back of the buckboard. Jessup stepped up to the prisoner then, holding a hood. He offered the hood to the young cowboy.

"No," Josh said, turning his head to one side. "When I meet my Maker, I want Him to see my face so that He may judge me innocent of any wrongdoin'."

"Have it your own way," Jessup growled. "You got 'ny last words?"

Josh looked out over the crowd. In the faces of those closest to the buckboard he saw an almost eager anticipation. In the faces of those farther back he saw pity, sorrow, even shame. Nowhere did he see a face that offered hope.

"I reckon not," Josh replied.

"Come on, Charlie, get it over with," one of the deputies shouted. "I want to see him dance."

Jessup held up his hand, then stepped toward the edge of the buckboard to shout his words to those who had already gathered and those who were now gathering to see what was going on: "I want it known by ever'body present that this here is a legal hangin', the prisoner havin' been tried an' found guilty in a court of law."

"A court of law," Doc Sweeny snorted under his breath. "There have been *lynchings* with more legal justification than this."

Though Doc Sweeny spoke only loudly enough for Miller and Appleby to hear him, Jessup must have sensed that he said something, for he looked, challengingly, toward the three men.

"How about any of you three men over there?" Jessup called. "Have you anything to say on behalf of this prisoner?"

"If we did have anything to say, would it make any difference?" Appleby asked.

"It would have no bearin' on the decision of this court," Jessup replied.

"Then we have nothing to say," Appleby said.

Jessup looked over at Muley and nodded. Muley put the thirteen-knot noose around Josh's neck. When that was done, Jessup turned to the prisoner. "Boy, I'm tellin' you this for your own good. Whenever the buckboard is pulled out from under you, if you'll let your neck be relaxed, it'll snap like a twig and ever'thing will be over in a second. Tighten up and it's likely to take a little longer. I've seen men tighten up their neck, then kick for near half an hour after they was hung."

Though Josh said nothing, he did nod in the affirmative.

Jessup and Muley jumped down from the buckboard. Jessup looked toward the front of the buckboard where the driver was sitting, holding the reins of the team. Jessup nodded, and the driver snapped the reins against the team, urging them forward. The buckboard pulled out from under Josh Speedwell and the crowd gasped as he was dragged off by the rope. He fell a short distance, then the rope stopped short. Perhaps Josh had taken Jessup's advice, for he didn't kick when he hit the bottom of the fall. In fact, except for the pendulum-like swing, there was no movement at all.

CHAPTER 6

Puxico, five days later

LATE IN THE AFTERNOON TWO NEW MEN came riding into town, whooping and shouting, and firing their pistols into the air. As always under such circumstances, the long-suffering citizens of Puxico could do nothing but shiver in fear and resignation, and pull back even deeper into the homes and businesses where they were taking refuge. How much longer, they wondered, could they bear up under such oppression?

From the second floor of the Miller General Mercantile Store, Jarred Appleby pulled the window shade to one side and looked down at the two new arrivals.

"What is it?" someone asked.

"It's nothing. Just a couple of riders comin' into town," Appleby replied. "They are new men, I think. At least, I haven't seen them before. They're just shootin' into the air."

"Even that is dangerous," Lem Miller complained. "A couple of weeks ago I had to replace a windowpane in this very room because one of those wild men started shootin' into the air."

"Be glad it was just a windowpane," one of the others said.

"Yes, but what if my wife or one of my children had been in here?" Miller asked.

"Lem is right. A man ought to be safe in his own home or place of business," Jake Suter said. "I'm tellin' you, we've got to do somethin'. It can't go on like this much longer."

"Well, now, gentlemen, that's why we're here," Appleby said. "I mean, as far as I'm concerned, hangin' that innocent cowboy last week, then claimin' it was a legal act . . . that's the last straw."

Appleby let the shade fall back in place, then returned to his chair to rejoin the others. Appleby was the general manager of the Consolidated Mining Company. Lem Miller was the owner of the Miller General Mercantile Store. Besides Appleby and Miller, there were four other men present in the room, all legitimate businessmen and leading citizens of Puxico. They were: Jake Suter, the town carpenter; Ed Alsup, owner of a leather-goods store; Parson

Sloan, the town preacher; and the town doctor, Lucas Sweeny. As Appleby had suggested, the six men were meeting to discuss the problems which had befallen their town, and to try and seek some solution.

"Perhaps if we did nothing," Parson Sloan suggested.

"Nothing? By God, we've tried doing nothing, and it doesn't work," Alsup said. "Excuse my language, Parson."

"No, that's not what I mean," the parson replied. "We haven't done nothing . . . I mean, actively done nothing."

"Parson, what in the Sam Hill are you talkin' about?" Appleby asked.

"Well, why does anyone come to a town in the first place?" Parson Sloan asked. "They come to town for the goods and services a town provides. Food, clothing, saddles, guns and ammunition, beer, whiskey, haircuts—everything that civilization offers. Suppose we didn't offer any such thing here. Suppose we got every merchant to agree to shut down his business."

"For how long?" Miller asked.

"For as long as it takes," Sloan replied. "When the outlaws can no longer get the things a town has to offer, perhaps they'll leave our town and go somewhere else."

"You mean be someone else's worry?" Appleby asked.

"Well, yes, in a manner of speaking," Sloan admitted.

"Maybe the parson's got a point there," Appleby suggested. "Why not give it a try?"

"And what about the townspeople during that time?" Miller asked. "I've got folks that depend on me. What are they supposed to do for food and clothing?"

"Yeah, and what about us merchants?" Alsup asked. "How are we supposed to make a living?"

"I didn't say it would be easy," Sloan said. "I just said it was a possibility."

"There's another thing to consider here. I've got three women who are expecting children," Doc Sweeny said. "Now I know babies have been comin' into this world long before there were doctors, but it looks like Mrs. Clark is goin' to have a difficult birth. What if she starts to deliver? Am I just supposed to stand by and do nothing?"

"Well, no, of course not," the parson stammered. "I mean, I wouldn't expect you to just let someone die."

"Yes, but that's just it, don't you see?" Alsup asked. "If we convince Parmeter over at the saloon to close down now, when truth to tell he's makin' more money than he ever has before . . ."

"But let's be fair to Parmeter," Suter said, quickly. "He told me the extra money he's makin' isn't even payin' for all the damage they're doin' over there . . . breakin' up the tables and chairs, bustin' out all the windows. I know all that's goin' on, because I've done a lot of repair work for him myself. He's as ready to have these men leave as any of us."

"Maybe so. But then that's all the more reason he needs the extra money he's makin'," Alsup continued. "And if he sees Doc here still treatin' folks, then he's goin' to feel like he has the right to continue to run his saloon. No, sir, I don't think it's goin' to work."

"Then what *are* we goin' to do?"

"Did any of you hear what happened over in Sundown last week?" Appleby asked.

"What? You mean the bank holdup?" Miller asked.

"Not just the bank holdup. It's what happened after that I'm talkin' about. The three that did it were caught. One was killed, and the other two was brought in. They already been tried—a legal trial, I might add—and they're goin' to be hung tomorrow."

"How'd they bring 'em in so fast? Did they get up a posse? Is that what you think we should do?" Suter asked. "Because if it is, I'm willin', but I don't know if we could get enough men who would be."

Appleby shook his head. "No, they didn't use a posse," he said. "One man brought them in."

"One man? Who?"

"Sam Slater."

"Sam Slater? Say, ain't he the one they call The Regulator?" Suter asked.

Appleby nodded. "That's him."

"I've heard tell he's nothin' but a killer his own self," Miller said.

"That may be," Alsup agreed. "But from what ever'one says, he ain't never killed a man that didn't need killin'."

"Look here," Doc Sweeny said. "Are you sayin' we should get The Regulator to come clean up our town?"

"I believe we should if we could."

"Do you think we can?"

"I don't know. Maybe if we made it worth his while, he would come," Appleby said. "After all, that is what he does for a living. He is a bounty hunter."

"Yes, but as far as I know, there's no bounty on any of these men. Leastwise, not enough of a bounty to make it worth his while."

"Maybe we could come up with the money ourselves," Appleby suggested. "I think I can speak for Consolidated Mining when I say we will offer one thousand dollars. Now, if we could raise that much money from the rest of the town, that would be two thousand dollars. That seems to me a generous enough sum to persuade Mr. Slater to come to our rescue."

"I'm willin' to come up with two hundred fifty," Miller said. "Alsup, if you can raise two hundred fifty, I think we can get that much out of Parmeter over at the saloon. That would only leave two hundred fifty for the whole rest of the town."

"Two hundred fifty is pretty dear for me

right now," Alsup complained. "Jessup come in and took a saddle yesterday that was worth a hundred fifty, easy. And you know what he give me for it? Twenty dollars. Twenty measly dollars, and that's all. Hell, it cost me damn near that much just to have it shipped out here, let alone what it cost me to buy it."

"Well, what are you tellin' me, Alsup? That you want stuff like that to keep on happenin'?" Miller asked.

Alsup shook his head. "No, by God, I don't," he said. "All right, I'll come up with two hundred and fifty dollars. Parson, you think you could raise the rest from your parishioners?"

Parson Sloan shook his head. "Gentlemen, do you hear what you are saying? You are saying that you are willing to pay a hired killer to come to town to kill these men."

"You're goddamn right that's what we're sayin'," Suter said.

"If we do that, it would make us no better than the men we are trying to eliminate, don't you see? We are resorting to the ways of violence."

"Yeah, well, Preacher, sometimes there just ain't no other way," Miller said. "Not too many years back, you might recollect, this whole country was pushed into violence. We fought us one hell of a war to preserve the Republic. I was just a young man from Ohio then, but I picked up a soldier's pack and I went off to do my duty. I was an artilleryman at Shiloh, Preacher. I seen enough violence to last me a lifetime. And I didn't go through all that to kowtow to a bunch of varmints like Charlie Jessup and his gang. No, sir. If we have to pay someone to come kill 'em, then I say better them than us. Now, are you in, or out?"

"I can't condone this," Parson Sloan said. He stood up and reached for his hat, then pulled it down low on his head. "Gentlemen, I will make no effort to stop you, or to get in your way. But, in all good conscience, I cannot actively take part in this. I won't solicit money for you, and I won't be a part of the committee that deems it necessary to employ a professional killer. If you'll excuse me?"

"I'm real sorry you feel that way, Parson Sloan," Appleby said. "I think that now, more than any other time, a town needs the moral guidance of a preacher."

"Moral guidance?" Parson Sloan repeated. He sighed, and shook his head. "I thought that was what I just tried to offer you. Good day, gentlemen."

The others watched Sloan go down the stairs, then heard the door down on the street open and shut.

"Ah, the hell with him. We don't need him anyway," Miller said.

"No, but it would have been good to have him support us," Appleby said.

"Hell, we've only got two hundred fifty more dollars to raise. We can do it without him."

"It isn't just the money," Appleby said. "His support would have lent a degree of moral credence to what we are plannin' to do. It would have gone a long way toward gettin' rid of any squeamishness some of the townspeople might have."

Across the street from the Miller General Mercantile Store, the two men who had just ridden into town a few minutes earlier were now in the Silver Strike Saloon. One of them, drinking whiskey from a bottle, walked over to look out across the top of the batwing doors onto the street. He took a long swallow, then wiped his mouth with the back of his hand.

"Hey, Bodine. Bodine, get over here and look at this," he said, laughing. "This is about the funniest-lookin' thing I ever seen."

Bodine, who also was drinking his whiskey from a bottle, was leaning against the bar.

"What you find so funny, Cooper?" Bodine asked.

"The hat this here fella is wearin'. Come over here and take a gander at it."

Bodine walked over to the batwing doors. "Where?" he asked.

"Hell, are you blind? It's right there," Cooper said. "Look at the crown of that hat. Look how low down the crown of that hat is. Why, I bet it don't come up more'n two inches from the top of the head. And now look at how wide the brim is.

You figure the fella that made that hat was drunk, or somethin'?"

"Naw, that fella's a preacher, that's all," Bodine said. He took a drink of his whiskey, then lowered the bottle. "Don't you see how he's all dressed in black, an' wearin' that funny collar? That's the kind of hats preachers sometime wear."

"Hell, I know'd he was a preacher," Cooper said. "I was just makin' comment on the hat, is all." He took another drink. "Bet I could shoot it off his head," he said.

"From how far?"

"From here."

Bodine measured the distance between the door of the saloon and the approaching preacher.

"The hell, you say," he said. "That crown's no more'n two inches high, and he's a good two hundred and fifty feet away."

"It'd be a hell of a shot, I admit, but ten bucks says I can do it," Cooper insisted, taking out his pistol. "I'm just goin' to let him get a little closer."

"All right, I'll take that bet. But you see the other end of that water trough?" Bodine said.

"Yeah, I see it. What about it?"

"That's too close. If you don't shoot it off before he gets there . . . the bet's off."

"Get your ten bucks ready," Cooper said, taking careful aim.

★ ★ ★

Back in the loft of Miller's Store, Jake Suter, feeling a need to stretch his legs, had gotten up and moved over to the window. He was watching the preacher walk down the street. Behind him he could hear the buzz of conversation as the others discussed how best to approach Sam Slater. They were trying to talk Doc Sweeny into being their messenger, believing that he was the one to whom Slater would most likely listen. But Doc Sweeny was having a difficult time being persuaded, because he was beginning to believe that perhaps Parson Sloan was right.

"How do we know we won't be jumpin' from the frying pan into the fire?" Doc asked the others. "Maybe this isn't such a good idea after all."

"Goddamnit, Doc, we've got to do somethin'," Miller insisted.

Suddenly Suter saw a flash and a puff of smoke emerge from just inside the saloon door. A second later he heard the shot and, at almost the same time, saw the preacher go down. Sloan fell on his back with his arms stretched out in the dirt on either side of him. His hat was off and his head was thrown back. Clearly visible, even from the second floor of Miller's store, was the large, bloody hole in the middle of Sloan's forehead.

"Oh, my God!" Suter said.

The others looked toward him.

"What is it, Jake? What'd you just see?"

"They just shot the preacher," Suter said in a quiet, tight voice.

"What?" Appleby asked. He rushed over to the window, followed by the others.

"My God! Who did it?"

"I don't know exactly," Suter said. "But I seen the puff of smoke. The shot come from inside the saloon."

Doc Sweeny started quickly down the stairs.

"Doc, where you goin'?"

"To see if I can do anything for the preacher," Doc Sweeny called back over his shoulder.

The others followed him down the stairs, then out into the street, though in truth, it was as much out of a sense of morbid curiosity as it was any desire to help. Actually, they already knew that the preacher was beyond help.

By the time they reached Sloan there were already a couple of dozen people gathered around the grisly scene. The way Sloan was lying, with his arms spread straight out to either side of him, reminded Appleby of Christ on the cross. He thought the symbolism was significant, though he didn't comment on it.

"Can you do anything for him, Doc?" Parmeter asked.

Doc Sweeny, who was squatted down beside the body, sighed and shook his head. "He was dead before he hit the ground," he said, raising up. "What the hell happened? Who shot him, and why?"

"I reckon I done it," Cooper said.

"Who are you?" Doc asked.

"The name is Cooper. Seamus Cooper. But I want you to know that it was a accident and I'm just real remorseful about it."

"An accident? An accident?" Doc Sweeny said. "Man, how do you accidentally shoot someone right between the eyes?"

"I bet Bodine here ten dollars I could knock off his funny little hat," Cooper said. "I reckon I missed. I don't understand it, neither. I had me a real good bead on it."

"You bet ten dollars?" Doc Sweeny said angrily. "You killed a man for ten dollars?"

"Take it easy, Doc," a new voice said. "You heard him say it was a accident."

When Doc Sweeny looked around, he saw that Jessup and his chief deputy, Muley, had come upon the scene. "Hello, Cooper, Bodine," Jessup said. "I heard you boys was comin' to join us. It's good to see you."

Cooper and Bodine shook Jessup's hand, and smiled broadly. "Sonofabitch!" Cooper said. "It's true then, ain't it? You are the sheriff over here!"

"That's right," Jessup said. "I'm also the judge. And, as the judge, I owe it to the good people of this town to see that justice is done here." He pointed to the preacher's body. "I'm afraid you two men are goin' to have to pay for this."

"Now, wait a minute, Charlie," Cooper said.

"I done told you it was a accident. And I told these here folks just how remorseful I am. Now that ought to be the end of it."

"Yeah, well, bein' sorry ain't quite enough," Jessup said. "I got to come up with some sort of penalty." He suddenly smiled. "I got it," he said. "What was it you said you was bettin'? Ten dollars?"

"Yeah, ten dollars."

"All right, that would make the pot a total of twenty dollars. I'll take it," Jessup said.

"Hold on, Charlie, that ain't hardly right," Bodine said. "The money's mine now—I won the bet. Besides which, I didn't shoot the sonofabitch, Cooper did."

"You didn't shoot him but you, . . . uh, what's that word?" Jessup asked. Then he smiled. "Oh, yeah, 'aided and abetted.' You aided and abetted this here accidental shootin', so you got to pay up just like Cooper here. I'll take the twenty dollars."

Grumbling, Bodine handed over the twenty dollars. "It don't seem right," he said. "We told you it was a accident."

"Yeah, well, accident or not, the preacher's dead and he's goin' to need a decent buryin'," Jessup said. He took the twenty dollars from Bodine, then handed it over to Doc Sweeny. "I tell you what, Doc," Jessup said. "You take this here money and see to it the preacher gets buried real proper." Jessup brushed his hands together, as if having just finished a difficult task. "There, now, that's all took care of, short and sweet. Come on back into the saloon, boys. I'll swear you in as my deputies, then we'll visit for a while."

When Jessup and his deputies left, there remained behind only those townspeople who were both curious enough and courageous enough to be out in the street.

"Deputies. Did you hear that?" someone asked, disgustedly. "Jessup's goin' to make them two galoots deputies."

"Yeah, so what? They ain't no different from any of the others," another answered.

By now the undertaker had also arrived, and he was looking down, solemnly, at the body.

"Will twenty dollars be enough to handle the buryin', Abner?" Doc Sweeny asked, handing over the money.

Abner waved the money aside. "Jake was just tellin' me that you're goin' to be goin' around town, collectin' money to hire someone to come help us out," he said. "You go ahead an' put that twenty dollars in the pot. I'll bury Parson Sloan for free."

"What do you say, Doc?" Appleby asked. "You still think the preacher was right?"

Doc Sweeny took one last look at the preacher, then shook his head.

"Get the rest of the money together," he said. "I'll be your messenger."

CHAPTER 7

WHEN DOC SWEENY RODE INTO THE LITTLE town of Sundown the next day, he thought they must be having a circus. The street was crowded with men, women, and children, most of whom were dressed in their Sunday finery. A medicine wagon was doing a brisk business at one end of the street, while elsewhere, vending kiosks had been set up to offer for sale sandwiches, beer, or candy.

"Lucinda! Lucinda, you get back here," an anxious mother called to a little girl who dashed out into the street. "Billy, go out there and get your sister!"

"Oh, Mom, Larry says he knows where there's a good spot in the loft of the livery. If I don't hurry, someone else will beat me to it," Billy complained.

"Go get your sister, I said," the mother repeated,

undaunted by the young man's complaint. "You want her to get runned over?"

Doc drove his buckboard and team past the medicine wagon. There were several men and women gathered around the wagon, listening to the pitchman give his spiel.

"Hey, Professor!" someone shouted from the crowd. "Do you reckon a bottle of your tonic will do them boys any good after they get hung?"

The others laughed.

"My friend," the pitchman replied, easily, "it might indeed, but far be it from me to thwart the intent of the law. No, sir, I do not intend to put it to the test."

The crowd laughed even harder.

A young towheaded boy hurried out to meet Doc's buckboard. He was holding up a paper.

"Mister, you want a souvenir program?" the boy asked. "They only cost a nickel."

Doc stopped his team. "Only a nickel?" He smiled at the boy. "Well, I guess I could afford one of those," he said, taking a coin from his pocket. "What is it a souvenir of?"

"Are you jokin' with me, mister?" the boy asked. "You mean you don't know about the double hangin' we're havin' here in Sundown?"

"You mean, that's what all this is?" Doc asked, taking in the crowd with a sweep of his hand. "All these people are here to see the hanging?"

"Sure. We ain't never had no hangin' here before," the boy said. "Leastwise, not one that was legal. They found Jim Lacey hangin' from a

tree couple of months ago, but they don't
nobody know, yet, who done that. This here
hangin' is all legal and proper. You can read all
about it in the program," the boy added. He
turned and started toward another part of the
crowd. "Program!" he shouted. "Get your souvenir program here!"

Doc looked at the program.

LEGAL HANGING!
of the Noted Outlaws
Terry Estes and Johnny Singleton
to take place in the town of
Sundown
On Tuesday, September 21st

SCHEDULE OF EVENTS:
Address by Territorial Lieutenant Governor,
the honorable T. Oliver Shipman
Songs by Methodist Church Choir
Address by the Reverend Lester W. Owens
Music by the Sundown Volunteer Fire Department Band
Reading of warrant of execution by
Sheriff Daniel Barkett
Order for execution to commence by
the honorable Judge Jeremiah Townsdale
Prayer by the Reverend Lester W. Owens
Last words by Terry Estes and Johnny Singleton
Hanging

Doc Sweeny contrasted the organized structure
of this legal hanging with the lynching he had

witnessed back in Puxico last week. The result of any hanging, be it legal or illegal, was the same, he knew. But there was something reassuring in the organization and structure of a legal hanging. Though he probably couldn't have articulated his thoughts, he knew that this structure offered some protection. Surely no one would be hanged in such a fashion unless he had already had the benefit of the fullest due process of law.

On the other hand, he thought, what happened in Puxico last week could have happened to just about anyone. Though he would not wish upon any man the ordeal of witnessing a hanging, he couldn't help but think it would be good if Miller and Appleby were over here now, so that they could see justice being carried out as it was supposed to be.

Doc parked his buckboard in a lot where dozens of other buckboards and wagons stood, then walked across the crowded street to the sheriff's office. To one side of the sheriff's building a couple of men were putting the finishing touches on the newly constructed gallows. A man who Doc figured must be the hangman was sitting on the side of the gallows, working with a rope. One rope had already been fashioned into a thirteen-knot noose and was lying, ominously, to one side.

There were a total of five men inside the building. Three were gathered around a desk, laughing and talking. The other two, who were much more solemn, were in the jail's only cell.

These, Doc assumed, were the condemned prisoners.

One of the three men around the desk looked up when Doc Sweeny came in.

"If you're lookin' for tickets to the hangin', you don't need any," he said. Sweeny saw that the man was wearing a badge on his vest. "Just go out there and find yourself a good place to stand."

"The street is so crowded now, I doubt there is anyplace to stand," one of the other men said.

The sheriff pointed to the cell. "Well, hell, that ain't no problem," he said. "I reckon either one of these boys would give up his place for you." He and the other two men around the desk laughed at his joke.

"I'm not here for the hanging," Doc Sweeny said.

"You ain't?" the sheriff asked. "What are you here for?"

"My name is Doctor Sweeny. I live over in Puxico."

"Puxico," the sheriff snorted. "Then I can see why you ain't interested in a hangin'. From what I hear, you folks had a hangin' of your own over there, last week."

"Hanging? Lynching, you mean," Doc Sweeny said.

"Lynching? That's a pretty strong charge," one of the men said. He was a short, fat man, wearing a three-piece suit with a gold watch chain stretched across the vest.

"Who are you?" Doc Sweeny asked.

"I am Judge Townsdale."

"Lynching may be a strong word, Judge, but it is, nonetheless, an accurate representation of what happened," Doc Sweeny said. "By the way, I understand it was The Regulator who brought these men in. Is that correct?"

"That's right."

"Good, then I'm not too late. I suppose he's out there, somewhere, waiting for the hanging?"

"May I inquire as to why you are interested in Sam Slater?" Judge Townsdale asked.

"It is my hope . . . rather, it is the hope of myself and several others in our community, that Mr. Slater can be persuaded to come to Puxico to, uh, bring peace to our town."

"Evidently, that's what you tried to do last week," Judge Townsdale said. "Bring peace to your town by hanging—or, as you suggest, by lynching—an outlaw."

"An outlaw? Judge, that boy was no more of an outlaw than I am," Doc said. "None of them were. They were just cowboys, that's all, come to town for a little relaxation. One of Jessup's deputies goaded two of them into a fight and they were killed. The boy they hanged was upstairs at the time. He didn't have anything to do with it."

"Then you do have a bad situation over there, I admit," Judge Townsdale said. "I wish my jurisdiction extended that far, but I would have to get approval from the federal court to come over there and intervene. And, I would have to have the support of the local sheriff."

"Jessup?"

"He is the sheriff."

"He is also the biggest problem."

"Then you see my dilemma," Judge Townsdale said.

"And you see ours. That's why I've come to speak with Mr. Slater."

"Well, you won't find Slater out there," Judge Townsdale said. "He never watches the hangings."

"You mean I've missed him?"

The judge shook his head. "No, I didn't say that. I just said you won't find him watching the hanging. In fact, he is still in town. He's waiting for the reward money to come through."

"Where is he? Has he taken a hotel room somewhere?"

"I think he has," the sheriff offered. "But you'll most likely find him over at the saloon."

"Thanks," Doc said.

The saloon was across the street and several buildings down the block. Doc pushed his way through the crowd, then stepped up onto the boardwalk. How total the town's fascination was with the upcoming hanging was especially evident in the saloon, for it was almost completely empty. None of the lanterns were lit and the interior was lighted only by the alternating bars of light and shadow which stabbed in through the slits in the window shutters and splashed in over the batwing doors.

Over in the shadows behind the bar a lone bartender stood, busily polishing glasses. In the darkest gloom of the farthest corner of the saloon there was another man, a single customer who was sitting at a table, staring into his glass. The customer looked up as Doc approached his table, and Doc saw the scar on his cheek. It matched the one Doc had heard described, so he knew this was the one they called The Regulator.

"Mr. Slater?" he asked.

"Just Sam will do," Sam said.

Doc pointed to one of the chairs around the table. "Do you mind if I join you?"

The chair slid out in invitation, and Doc saw that Sam had pushed it out with his foot.

"Thank you."

"You have the money?" Sam asked.

"Yes," Doc said. "How did you . . .? Oh, you mean the reward money for the two men who are about to hang, don't you. Uh, no, I don't have it."

"What money are you talking about?"

"I, uh, have a proposition for you, Sam," Doc said.

Sam took a swallow of his drink, and studied Doc over the rim of his glass. "What sort of proposition?" he asked, putting the glass back down.

"My name is Doctor Sweeney. I represent the good citizens of Puxico," Doc said. "Have you ever heard of it?"

"Yeah, I've heard of it."

"We used to mine silver in Puxico," Doc said. "When that played out, we switched to copper. In a lot of ways, that was even better. Copper tends to attract more solid citizens than gold or silver. At least that was what we thought. Instead, Puxico is hell on earth. There are beatings and frequent killings. Decent men are being cheated and robbed of their stores and businesses. The good people are too frightened to leave their homes. We are being turned into a ghost town by a bunch of outlaws."

"Go to the sheriff," Sam suggested.

Doc shook his head. "You don't understand, Sam. The sheriff and his deputies *are* the outlaws. Why, they lynched an innocent man last week, then tried to pass it off as a legal hanging."

Sam took another swallow of his drink. "Why are you comin' to me with this?"

"Well I—that is, we—thought you might be willing to help us if, uh, the price was right. I don't know exactly what your price is, Mr. Slater. But we have raised two thousand dollars. The money is for you if you will . . ."

"Kill the sheriff and his deputies?" Sam asked.

"Well, no, not exactly."

"Then what, exactly?" Sam asked. "You know these men. If they have a good thing goin' over there in Puxico, and it sounds to me like they do, do you think they are goin' to just go away?"

"Probably not," Doc admitted.

"And if they don't go away, how am I to take care of the situation?"

"I don't know," Doc admitted.

In the streets outside the saloon the crowd noises had stopped and there could now be heard the shouted words of someone making a speech:

"A code of justice . . . and decent, God-fearing, law-abiding men to administer that justice . . ."

Sam finished his drink. "The only way I could take care of it would be to kill the sheriff and as many of his deputies as it took to get the others to leave," he said. "Am I right?"

"Yes," Doc said, quietly.

"I want to get this straight, Doc," Sam said. "I want you to understand that you and the 'good' citizens of Puxico are attemptin' to hire me to kill for you."

"I . . . I guess if you want to put it like that."

"How else should I put it?"

"No way else, I guess."

The speech was over outside, and now a choir was singing hymns:

Oh worthy Judge eternal!
When Thou dost bid us come,
Then open wide the gates of pearl,
And call Thy servants home.

Sam smiled, though the smile never reached his eyes. "Well, I'll save your conscience for you," he said. "I won't do it."

"You . . . you won't accept the job?"

"That's what I said."

"Why not? Is it not enough money? Because if that's the problem, maybe we can raise more. How much more do we need?"

"It isn't the money," Sam said. "I'm not a hired killer."

"But you . . . you are a bounty hunter, aren't you?" Doc asked.

"A bounty hunter, Doc, not a bounty killer," Sam said. "I've killed when I've had to. I bring them in when I can. What's going on outside should be proof of that."

The hymns were over now, and another speech was in progress:

"*. . . to bring law to the lawless, and to take our place, in dignity, upon the stage of man.*"

"What *is* goin' on outside?" Doc asked. "The men you brought in alive are about to be killed, aren't they? What difference did it make whether you did it or whether it is done by the law? They are just as dead. In fact, given their choice, they would probably rather they had been killed by you. That way, at least they wouldn't have had to go through this macabre circus."

Sam nodded. "I'll grant that you have a point there," he said. "They probably would have been better off." He sighed. "But that isn't my decision to make." He got up and walked over toward the bar to pour himself another drink.

Now, from outside, there was band music.

"Listen, Sam, do you think it's easy for me to come to you with this proposition?" Doc called over to him. "I'm a doctor, for God's sake. Do you know what that means? That means I have spent my entire life tryin' to save others. And now, here I am, offerin' you blood money to kill other human beings. My God, man, this is a violation of all that I believe in, of everything that I hold dear. But, I swear to you, sir, if ever there was a man who needed killin', it is Charlie Jessup."

Sam looked back around, quickly. "Did you say Charlie Jessup?"

"Yes," Doc said. "We—that is, the Consolidated Mining Company—hired him to guard the silver shipments back when they were still mining silver. When they switched from silver to copper, they no longer had need of his services, so they let him go. Only, he didn't leave town. Instead, he browbeat the city council into making him the sheriff. It has been hell since then."

The band music stopped.

Sam turned back to the bar and raised the glass to his mouth. "I don't know who it was, but it was a wise man who once said that most men create their own hell. I suppose that is true for towns, too."

"All right, all right, I'll admit, we brought Charlie Jessup into town," Doc Sweeny said. "But should everyone suffer for that? The women and children, the innocent? Sam, you don't know what we've been goin' through."

"I'm sorry," Sam said. "I can't help you."

During their last few exchanges there were a few more words audible from outside, concluding with these:

"... *hanged by the neck until dead.*"

"Then, if there is nothing I can do to change your mind . . .?" Doc said in one final plea.

"Nothing," Sam said. By now Sam had turned his back to the doctor and stood at the bar, staring morosely into his drink.

"I'll be goin' then." Doc looked pointedly at Sam for a long moment, but Sam never bothered to look around. Outside, the preacher was saying a final prayer for the condemned:

"*Unto God's gracious mercy and protection we commit thee. The Lord bless thee, and keep thee. The Lord make his face to shine upon thee, and be gracious unto thee. The Lord lift up his countenance upon thee, and give thee peace, both now and evermore. Amen.*"

After Doc left the saloon he pushed his way through the crowd. It was strangely silent now, compared to the earlier circus atmosphere. One of the outlaws had just been invited to speak. Doc looked around and saw him standing there with his arms bound stiffly by his sides and his legs tied together.

"As I look around here," the outlaw said, "I see very many enemies, and very few friends. You youngsters, when you grow old, remember me to your grandchildren. Those memories of me are all that will be left of Terry Estes."

The other outlaw declined the invitation to speak. Doc found his buckboard, then turned his team around and started out of the lot, keeping the activity in the street behind him. A moment later he heard the thumping sound of the trapdoors falling open, then the collective gasp of the crowd. After that there was a moment of silence.

Doc knew that the two men were now swinging, silently, from the ends of the ropes, but he made no effort to look around to see them. Instead, he rode to the far end of the street, then turned onto the road leading back to Puxico. Not once did he look back.

CHAPTER 8

IT WAS AFTER DARK BY THE TIME DOC returned to Puxico. He could hear the town even before he saw it—the trill of a piano, the breaking of glass, then a woman's high-pitched scream, followed by a man's basso laughter. These were the sounds of a town in its death throes, and Doc slumped down in his seat as he let the team plod along over the familiar trail. As he drew closer he could see the shine of lights from the saloons.

Wearily and dejectedly, he headed for the livery stable. As he pulled his team to a stop, he heard someone call to him from the shadows.

"Doc?"

"Who is it?" Doc asked, staring into the darkness.

"It's me, Appleby," Appleby said, walking into a little patch of light thrown by the lantern on the front of the stable. "I thought I'd wait for you to come back. The others are over at Miller's waitin' for me to bring you over."

Doc sighed. "I wish I had somethin' to bring them," he said.

"Didn't you find Slater?"

"Oh, yes, I found him all right," Doc said. "But it didn't do any good. He won't help us."

"Why not? Is it not enough money? Look, Doc, if we have to raise more money, we can do it. I'll write a letter to the mine owners, explainin' what's goin' on around here. In a way, it's the mine's fault anyway. If we hadn't hired Jessup in the first place, none of this would be happenin' now."

"I wish I could tell you that more money is all we need," Doc said. "But that isn't it. Slater won't do it, no matter how much money we offer him." Doc began unhitching his team and Appleby helped.

"Why not?" Appleby asked from his side of the team.

"He says what we're doin' is offering to pay him to be our killer."

"Yeah, I guess it is," Appleby said. "What's wrong with that?"

"What's wrong with that is that Slater doesn't consider himself a hired killer."

"What the hell does he consider himself?"

"A bounty hunter," Doc said.

"Hell, ever'body knows there ain't no difference between a bounty hunter and a hired killer."

"Evidently, there is a difference," Doc said. "Perhaps to us it is a subtle difference, but to Slater it is very real." By now the team was unhitched and Doc and Appleby turned them in to the corral. Both horses went immediately to the hayrick, where they began feeding. "I don't know," Doc added. "Maybe Slater is right. Maybe we have no business hirin' someone to kill for us."

"Come on, let's get over to Miller's to see the others," Appleby said. "They're waitin' to hear from us, but I'm sure not lookin' forward to tellin' 'em what you found out."

As the two men walked across the dark street, headed for the mercantile store, Bodine, who had been in the shadows all along, spit out his chew of tobacco, then wiped his mouth. When Doc and Appleby were far enough out into the dark so that he couldn't be seen, he started toward the Silver Strike. He was pretty sure Jessup would want to hear this.

The saloon was lighted by one huge, bright chandelier, as well as by a dozen or so kerosene lanterns. The bar was crowded and the tables were full. At least half a dozen of the men were wearing the badges of deputy. The others, while not officially deputies, were nevertheless taking advantage of the "wide-open" conditions of the town. Some, Bodine knew, were petty criminals, not well enough known to have to be on the run, but unable, or unwilling, to adjust to conditions in a normal town. Puxico was perfect for them. Here, there was no such thing as disturbing the peace, or public drunkenness.

Charlie Jessup was sitting at a table in the back corner of the saloon. He called this table his "office," and no one could sit at it without his express invitation. There were three others at his table now—a bar girl who had pulled her chair so close to his that her leg was lying across his lap, and two men, both of whom were studying the cards they were holding.

"Are you boys goin' to bet, or are you just goin' to sit there with your thumbs up your asses?" Jessup asked.

"I'm foldin'," one of the men said, throwing his cards in.

"Yeah, me too," the other followed. He, too, laid down his cards.

"Shit," Jessup said, raking in the pot. "You boys don't even make it fun." He looked up at Bodine. "What about you, Bodine? You want to play?"

"I ain't got enough money, yet," Bodine answered.

"Well then, what are you doin' over here?"

"I heard somethin' a while ago that I thought you might want to know," Bodine said.

"What's that?"

"Did you know the townspeople has got themselves together and raised enough money to hire 'em a bounty hunter?" Bodine said. "I think they wanted him to come to town and run us out."

Jessup chuckled. "Just one bounty hunter?" he said. "They must think he's one hell of a man." He had shuffled the cards and was beginning to redeal.

"They was talkin' like he was," Bodine said. "But he can't be too much. Leastwise, I ain't never heard of the sonofabitch."

"Who is it?" Jessup asked.

"Somebody named Slater."

Jessup stopped dealing and looked squarely at Bodine. "Who did you say?"

"Somebody named Slater," Bodine repeated. "I didn't get his first name. Anyhow, it don't matter. He's not comin'." Bodine chuckled. "I reckon he showed yellow."

"I've heard Sam Slater called lots of things," Jessup said. "But I've never heard The Regulator called yellow."

Rufus Colby was playing cards at a nearby table, and he chuckled. "You afraid of The Regulator, are you, Jessup?"

"You aren't?"

"Nope," Colby said, easily. He took the makings from his shirt pocket and began rolling a cigarette. "I figure he puts on his pants pert' near like anyone else."

"It ain't the way he puts on his pants that makes him dangerous," Jessup said.

"Well, don't be frightened, Jessup," Colby said smugly. "If you want me to, I'll take care of Salter for you."

The other deputies laughed, nervously, and Jessup glared at Colby.

"Oh, I'm not frightened, Colby," Jessup said. "I don't plan to go out of my way to run across him, but I'm not frightened."

"Maybe you think you can't beat him," Colby said, licking the cigarette paper, then tamping it closed. "I know I can."

"Colby, when you talk like that . . . it makes it sound as if you think you can beat me."

Colby lit his cigarette, then squinted through the cloud of smoke.

"I can," he said.

There was a sudden scraping of tables and chairs as everyone moved out of the way of the two men.

"Do you want to try right now?" Jessup asked, coldly, calmly.

Colby had faced many men, but he was used to seeing fear in their eyes and was always able to use that fear to his advantage. Jessup, however, was showing absolutely no fear whatever . . . and that lack of fear gave Colby pause. For the first time in his life he had an inkling of what others must feel. He wasn't exactly afraid of Jessup . . . but he didn't have total confidence that he would come out the better in any encounter between the two of them.

Slowly, deliberately, he took a puff from his cigarette, forcing himself to remain calm. He smiled insincerely.

"Now, why would I want to do something like that?" he asked. "You're the sheriff here, and I've a good thing goin', bein' your deputy. Besides that, I always figured we were friends. Friends don't go around throwin' down on friends, do they?"

"Colby, sometimes you have a funny way of talkin' to your friends," Jessup said.

Colby forced a chuckle. "Well," he said. "You might say that I'm a funny kind of a guy."

During the exchange of words between Jessup and Colby, the music and laughter stopped, and the loud conversation stilled. Jessup, now noticing the quiet, spoke out loud.

"What is it?" Jessup asked. "What's got into ever'one?"

"Nothing, Charlie," Muley said. "Nothing at all."

"Well, get on back to your drinkin' an' card playin'. There ain't nothing about to happen here that I can't handle."

"Yeah," Colby added. "Me an' Charlie was just havin' a friendly conversation about The Regulator, that's all."

"I been meanin' to ask, Charlie. Just who is

this 'Regulator' anyway?" Muley inquired. "I mean, he's just one man, ain't he?"

"That's right," Colby answered. "He's just one man."

"Colby, you keep talkin' about Slater like maybe you have his number. Let me ask you this. Have you ever tangled with him?" Jessup asked.

"No," Colby admitted. "I don't reckon anyone has who has lived to tell the tale. That's what makes him such a bogeyman."

"I know someone who has tangled with him . . . and who has lived to tell the tale," Jessup said.

"Who?"

"Me."

"You?" Colby asked. "I thought you were saying you didn't want to run across him again."

"I don't, particularly," Jessup answered. "You ever hit a hornets' nest with a stick?"

Colby chuckled. "Can't say as I have," he said.

"Well, if you were ever to do that once, you'd have more sense than to do it again," Jessup said. "That's what I did with Slater. I hit a hornets' nest with a stick."

"What happened?"

"What happened was, I shot him once, but I didn't finish him off," Jessup said. "I left him out there for the buzzards, only the buzzards threw him back."

"You . . . you mean you beat him?" Colby asked, visibly impressed by Jessup's revelation.

"I didn't exactly beat him," Jessup admitted. "I shot the sonofabitch from ambush."

"Why didn't you finish him off?"

"I knew that I only hurt him," Jessup said. "Some creatures, like bears, mountain lions, and The Regulator, you don't get close to when they're just wounded."

"What are you going to do if he comes?" Colby asked. "You're goin' to have to get close to him."

"He ain't comin'," Jessup said.

"He ain't? I thought that's what all this was about."

"That's 'cause you listened with your ass instead of your ears," Jessup growled. "Tell him, Bodine."

"I overheard the doctor and another fella talkin' down at the livery a little while ago," Bodine said. "Seems like they sent for Slater and they tried to pay him to come, but he wouldn't do it."

"Hell no, he wouldn't do it," Payson, another deputy, said. "He's afraid of Jessup!"

"Yeah! Let's hear it for Jessup!" Muley said.

All the deputies cheered then, except for Colby, who took a drink of his beer.

"Jessup, you got my vote to be sheriff as long as you want the job," one of the other deputies said.

"I don't need your vote, Simmons," Jessup

said, dryly. "Hell, I voted for myself. That's all the vote I need."

While the others laughed uproariously, Colby took a final puff from his cigarette.

CHAPTER 9

IT WAS NEARLY NOON THE NEXT DAY, AND
Seamus Cooper had been dry all morning. He
wanted a drink, but he didn't have any money
and that created a problem. If he had wanted to
eat, all he would have had to do would be to go
into the Railroad Cafe and order it with a
promise to "pay later." His deputy's badge gave
him that authority. There were any number of
other goods and services he could "purchase" in
town with the promise to pay later, just because
he was one of Jessup's deputies.

Those privileges did not extend to whiskey or
beer, though, because Jessup had made himself
a partner in the saloon. Jessup got a cut from
every drink that was sold, which meant that the

drinks had to be sold for cash to everyone, including the deputies.

That was the bad side. The good side was that it wasn't very difficult for a deputy to get money . . . at least enough money to buy a drink. All he had to do was collect a little "personal tax." This personal tax was the only way the deputies had of being paid, and they were responsible for collecting it themselves. When Jessup had set up that system, he'd also explained how it was to work.

"If you take everything they have at the point of a gun," Jessup had told his deputies, "it would be robbery. But if you only take a small amount, it will be taxation, and the citizen will be grateful for what you have left him."

There were other rules which more or less governed the behavior of the deputies. For example, in order not to kill the geese that were laying the golden eggs, a citizen of the town was not to be taxed twice in the same day. That meant that if one of the other deputies got to someone before Cooper did, Cooper was out of luck.

Jessup, of course, didn't have to tax anyone, directly. In addition to his "liquor tax" he also got a business tax from each of the merchants. Although he shared a portion of his liquor and business taxes with his number one and number two deputies, Muley and Colby, he kept the lion's share for himself. He was well on his way to becoming a wealthy man, without any fear of running afoul of the law.

Cooper was sitting on a chair on the sidewalk in front of Chin Ho's Laundry. From behind him, he could hear the singsong chatter of Chinese at work and smell the sharp odor of strong lye soap. Chin Ho, like the other business owners of the town, was exempt from the personal tax. The business tax he and the others paid to Jessup took care of that. Otherwise, Cooper would have already raised some money from Chin Ho, Lem Miller, or Clem Bell, the barber, for all three had walked by Cooper's vantage point since he'd taken his seat earlier this morning.

Cooper had his chair tipped back against the ripsawed boards which made up the false front of the laundry. His feet were wrapped around the front legs of the chair and his hat was pulled down low over his eyes. By now the sun was almost dead overhead, so that there were no shadows on the street. This was the hottest time of the day, which meant that most of the town's citizens would stay out of the sun as much as they could. The other deputies were back in the saloon drinking beer and playing cards.

Cooper heard the hollow, clumping sounds of a single rider and he looked toward the east to see a horseman coming into town. He smiled. If this man was just coming into town then it was a cinch he hadn't been taxed yet. This one belonged to him.

Cooper tipped his chair forward, then stood

up and watched as the rider came into town. Just across the street from the Chinese laundry, the rider pulled up, then dismounted, in front of the Model Barbershop. As he was tying his horse off at the hitching rail, he was met by Clem Bell, the barber.

"Yes, sir?" Clem Bell asked, standing out on the boardwalk in front of his shop. "Would you be wanting a haircut and a shave?"

"Yes," the rider grunted.

"That'll be two bits," the barber answered.

The rider flipped the barber a quarter, then went into the barbershop and took his seat in the single chair. Cooper stayed where he was for a moment, watching as the barber stretched out the chair, then wrapped hot towels around the customer's face. That was when he decided to go over and talk to the stranger.

"Howdy," Cooper said as he stepped inside the barbershop.

The man, whose face was wrapped in towels except for his eyes, opened one eye.

"Howdy," he replied.

"Do you see this here star?" Cooper asked, pointing to the badge on his vest. By now, Jessup had appointed so many deputies that he had run out of official stars. As a result, the one on Cooper's chest was a crude affair, fashioned from tin by the local blacksmith.

"Not much of a star," the customer grunted.

"Yeah? Well, don't let the looks of it fool you

none," Cooper replied. "'Cause I'm just as much a deputy as anyone else."

"Well, if that's what you want to be, I'm proud for you," the customer said.

Cooper stroked his chin. This conversation wasn't going exactly as he had planned.

"You ain't gettin' my drift, mister," Cooper said. "What I'm gettin' at is, as a deputy, I'm duly empowered to collect a tax. So, I reckon I'll just be collectin' from you. It's goin' to cost you two dollars to live here."

"I don't aim to live here," the man in the chair replied. "I'm just passin' through."

"It don't matter none whether you plan to live here or not," Cooper said. "As long as you are here, you are enjoyin' the protection of the sheriff and all his deputies. Now, don't you think that's somethin' worth payin' for?"

"Not particularly."

"Mister," Cooper said in a gruffer voice. "I don't seem to be gettin' through to you, do I? I'm here to collect a tax!"

"If it's all the same to you, I guess I'll just pass on the tax, and the protection."

Cooper drew his gun. "Now, I can't let you do that," he said. "You see, if I let you get away with not payin' your taxes, why then, the others might think they can try the same thing. Now, you can make it easy on yourself. You can fork over that two dollars like I told you, or . . ." He let the sentence hang.

"Or what?"

"Or I reckon I could just sift some lead through you, and take ever'thing you got," Cooper said.

"You plannin' on killin' me for two dollars?"

"It ain't the money, it's the principle of the thing," Cooper said. "I wouldn't be killin' you for two dollars. I'd be killin' you just to show ever'one else that you can't get away with not payin' up when you're told." He cocked the pistol and pointed it at the customer's head. "Now, what's it goin' to be, mister? Two dollars, or a hole in your head?"

The little barbershop was suddenly filled with the sound of an exploding cartridge. The apron that had been spread over the customer puffed up as a bullet tore through it . . . from the inside out. The shot left a tiny, brown ring of fire which blazed for an instant, then went out.

After passing through the apron, the bullet hit Cooper in the chest, tore through his heart, then exited just above his left shoulder blade, leaving a quarter-sized wound. The impact propelled Cooper through the door of the barbershop with such force that the door was torn from its hinges. Though he was already dead, the reflex action of his trigger finger caused his own pistol to discharge, firing harmlessly into the board sidewalk in front of the shop. Cooper fell back, faceup, off the edge of the sidewalk, landing with his head down in the dirt and his legs still up on the sidewalk itself. A spreading stain of blood soaked the front of his shirt.

The customer stood up from the barber chair and

pulled off the punctured apron, then unwrapped the towel from around his face. Fingering the purple lightning-flash scar on his cheek, he stepped outside to look down at Cooper's body. When he saw that Cooper was dead, he went back into the barbershop and retook his place in the chair.

The sound of the gunshot brought several people to the barbershop. The first ones to arrive were the merely curious . . . shopkeepers and citizens. Amazingly, none of those who came were wearing badges. Apparently, not even a gunshot could get the deputies out into the heat of midday.

One of the citizens who came hurrying toward the sprawled outlaw was Doc Sweeny. As he got close enough to see who it was, however, he slowed his pace. By the time he got there he was at a leisurely walk. Without even bending over, he kicked at the sole of Cooper's boot.

"What about it, Doc?" someone asked.

"This one, I don't mind pronouncin' dead," Doc Sweeny replied, and there was a nervous ripple of laughter from the others.

"Who did this?" Doc asked the barber.

"He did," the barber said, pointing with shaking hands to the customer inside.

"Mister," Doc called. "Don't know why the sheriff or none of his deputies showed up to see what the shooting was about, but if you got any sense, you'll ride on now, while you have the chance. With our gratitude," he added.

"Yeah," several other voices agreed.

The customer, who had put the towel around his face a second time, now stood up and removed the towel again. "I haven't even gotten my shave yet," he said.

"You!" Doc Sweeny gasped.

"Who is it, Doc?" someone asked quietly.

"It's the fella we were talkin' about," Doc said. "It's Sam Slater."

"Yesterday, you were tryin' to get me to come over. Today, you're tryin' to run me off," Sam said.

"No, sir," Doc Sweeny said. "We're not tryin' to run you off. Not by a long shot. You're welcome to stay as long as you want."

"Not only that, you've got the run of the town," Appleby put in.

Sam looked at Appleby. "Seems to me like that's how you folks got into trouble in the first place," he said. He sat back down in the barber chair. "I don't want you to get the wrong idea. I'm not takin' your offer. The only thing I want right now is a shave and a haircut."

Sam let Clem Bell put the apron on him. When the barber saw the brown-ringed hole in the apron, and thought again of what had just happened right in front of him, he got nervous. As he raised the razor to Sam's jaw his hand was shaking, visibly. Sam reached up to grab him by the wrist.

"I want my whiskers cut, not my throat," he said.

"Yes, sir," Bell replied. He took a couple of slow, deep breaths. "I'll be okay now."

"Well, how . . . how long are you goin' to stay?" Appleby asked.

"I haven't decided yet," Sam replied. "And I don't want to decide on an empty stomach. Where's the best place to get a meal?"

"The Railroad Cafe," Bell said quickly. "Uh, my wife runs it," he added.

"Your wife? Good," Sam said, leaning back in the barber chair. "I reckon I won't have to worry about you cuttin' my throat then. You wouldn't want your wife to lose a customer now, would you?"

Bell laughed more heartily than the joke called for.

"My wife lose a customer," he said as he began shaving Sam again, his hand somewhat more steady now. "That's a good one. Yes, sir, that's a good one."

CHAPTER 10

CHARLIE JESSUP WAS IN BED WITH ONE OF the whores, in his room upstairs and at the rear of the Silver Strike Saloon. He was just at that critical point, when he heard someone pounding on his door.

"Charlie! Charlie, you all finished in there? Charlie, open up!"

Jessup recognized Muley's voice. The interruption caused him to lose his concentration and he fell to one side of the girl, breathing hard in anger and frustration.

"I don't know what all the poundin' on that door's about, Muley," Jessup barked. "But it had better be good. It had better be damn good."

"Seamus Cooper just got hisself kilt!" Muley said.

Jessup swung his legs over the side of the bed, then looked over at the girl. With a modest smile, she pulled the sheet up to cover her breasts. Though the heavy green shade was pulled all the way down on his window, enough of the outside light slipped in around the edges so that the room was in shadows, giving the illusion, if not the reality, of coolness. With a sigh, Jessup ran his hand through his tousled hair, then walked over to open the door. Muley started to come in, but Jessup held him out in the hallway and talked through the crack in the barely opened door.

"Now, what's this about Cooper gettin' hisself kilt?" Jessup asked.

"It's just like I said," Muley replied. "Seems Cooper braced one of the town's citizens to collect some personal tax and the citizen killed him."

"Who did it?"

"I don't know," Muley admitted. "And to tell you the truth, I don't really much care. I just told you 'cause I figured you'd want to know. But I can't see goin' and makin' no big deal over it. Hell, ole Cooper wasn't worth a pound o' shit in the first place. Good riddance, is what I say."

"That ain't the point," Jessup growled. "If one of the good citizens of this town can kill Cooper and get away with it, then someone else might figure they can kill Bodine, then Payson, then Colby, then maybe even you, Muley. And after you, why, they might even want to kill me. You ever looked at it like that?" Jessup asked.

"No, I reckon not," Muley admitted.

"Yeah, well, that's why I'm the sheriff and you're the deputy. All right, never mind. Somethin' like that happens, folks can't keep quiet about it too long. We'll find out soon enough who it was. You just get on back to your card game and let me be."

"Okay, Charlie," Muley said. He started back, then turned around. "Oh, and I'm sorry 'bout interruptin' you like I done. Did you get finished?"

"That ain't none of your goddamned business," Jessup growled, slamming the door.

He turned back to the girl, who was still patiently waiting, naked, on the bed. He tried to take up where he left off and the girl was willing, but he was unable to perform. Finally, in a frustrated and impotent rage, he pushed the girl out of his bed.

"Get up!" he said, angrily. "Get up and get out of here!"

"I'm sorry, honey," the girl said.

"Sorry? You should be sorry, you worthless whore."

The girl reached for her clothes and started to get dressed.

"Get out!" Jessup said.

"I just want to get dressed," the girl complained.

"Get dressed somewhere else," Jessup growled. "I don't want to look at your ugly face anymore." He opened the door and shoved her, naked and protesting, out into the hall. When she saw Colby walking down the hall, she let out a little shout and made a desperate attempt to cover herself as she ran toward her own room.

"Hell, Annie, it ain't like I ain't seen you before," Jessup heard Colby call. "You was sharin' my bed just two nights ago!" Colby laughed as he clumped down the stairs.

Jessup had been unable to perform more than once now, and he was beginning to get a little worried about it. It wasn't something he wanted anyone to know about, and he had sworn all the girls to secrecy, threatening to do serious bodily harm to anyone who talked.

Jessup got dressed, then went downstairs to have a little lunch. He saw Colby sitting in his accustomed spot at the table next to the one where he always sat. More and more now, Colby was beginning to get on his nerves, and he wished he had never agreed to take him on as a deputy.

"I seen you throwin' Annie out of your room," Colby said. "What's wrong? Things didn't go too good for you?"

"What are you talkin' about?"

"Most of the time, when a man has a good time with a woman, he treats her a little better than to just throw her out like that." Colby chuckled. "Hell, you didn't even give her time to put on her clothes."

"Colby, you talk too goddamn much," Jessup growled.

Sam Slater had taken the barber's advice as to where to get a good meal, so that, at the same time Jessup was eating at the Silver Strike Saloon, Sam was having lunch at the Railroad Cafe. The news of Sam's encounter with Seamus Cooper had preceded him to the Railroad Cafe. As a result, people tended to give him a wide berth, stepping out of his way or purposely taking a table as distant from his as they could. That was fine with Sam, who had always been pretty much of a loner anyway. He ordered ham, eggs, fried potatoes, and coffee from the attractive woman who waited on his table, then ate his meal in silence.

Sam saw a man, woman, and young girl come into the cafe and take a table. The man was carrying a couple of large carpetbags.

"What if the train comes while we're in here, Papa?" the little girl asked. "If it comes while we're eatin', why, we'll miss it, and then we won't get to see Auntie Em."

"We have a whole hour yet," the girl's father replied. "That's plenty of time for us to eat."

"Are you going on a trip, Mr. Johnson?" one of the other customers asked.

"It's more than a trip, Jeb," Johnson replied. "We're movin' back to Missouri."

"You mean to say you're leavin' Puxico?" Jeb asked. "But no, Ben, why? You own the only hardware store in town. Folks need you."

"I don't own a hardware store," Johnson growled. "What I own is a supply depot where the sheriff and his deputies can get anything they want, anytime they want, without paying anything close to what it's worth. Besides which, they've scared away all the legitimate customers. No, the question isn't why am I goin'. The question is why anyone else is stayin'. All the merchants are goin' through the same thing."

"But most folks are stickin' it out, Ben. It can't be like this forever."

"It ain't just the stealin'," Mrs. Johnson put in. "It's the killin' too. Why, I heard there was another killin' just this mornin'."

"Yes'm, there was," Jeb said. "Seamus Cooper got himself killed. You recall him, don't you, Ben? He's the one who killed Parson Sloan. It's good riddance, I say."

"Yes, I know who Cooper is," Johnson replied. "And I agree with you, it's good riddance."

"It would have been even better if they had killed each other," Mrs. Johnson added.

Jeb, who knew that Sam was listening to every word, cleared his throat and glanced toward Sam's table.

"But I suppose it doesn't really matter," Mrs. Johnson continued, not understanding Jeb's signal. "Whoever killed Cooper today will probably get himself killed tomorrow. You reap what you sow, they say, and the proof was never more in the pudding than the fact that the man who killed our parson just got himself killed."

Jeb cleared his throat again, more loudly this time than before, then glanced, pointedly, at Sam's table. By now Ben Johnson realized what Jeb was doing, and when he too looked over toward the table, he recognized Sam from the description he had heard this morning from those who were telling the tale of the great barbershop shootout.

"That's enough, Stella," he said, putting his hand on his wife's arm.

"Well, you know I'm right, Ben Johnson," Stella replied.

"I said that's enough, woman," Ben growled again.

"What your husband is tryin' to tell you, ma'am, is that I'm the one who killed Cooper," Sam said, getting up from his meal. He smiled, disarmingly. "But you are quite correct when you say 'You reap what you sow.' Nobody knows that better than someone in my profession."

With a slight nod, Sam left the cafe, followed by the wide eyes of every patron in the place.

"What does he mean 'in his profession'?" Sam overheard Mrs. Johnson ask. "What is his profession?"

"He's a bounty hunter, Mrs. Johnson," Jeb answered. "That's the fella they call The Regulator."

It was always that way with Sam. Anytime he found himself in establishments of normal commerce, such as restaurants, mercantile stores, or railroad and stage depots, he would be around ordinary people. And when he was around ordinary people, he was acutely aware of the great gulf that separated him from civilized society. It was that way even though his profession, as brutal as it was, as distasteful to society as it might be, was very necessary. Without Sam Slater and men like him, the thin line of lawmen who attempted to keep peace in the West would have been strained beyond capacity.

Leaving the restaurant, Sam walked down the street toward the Silver Strike Saloon. He was always much more comfortable in saloons than he was anywhere else, because saloons were the great melting pots of society. Here, one might find an affluent businessman having a social drink with friends while next to them the town drunk lay passed out on the floor. Here, too, the law-abiding and the lawless met on common ground. It was only in saloons that Sam did not feel like such an outcast.

The Silver Strike was very busy, with most of the tables filled by drinking customers, though there were card games in session at three of them. Two of the games were penny-ante games, but there was one which was for much larger stakes.

Sam stepped up to the bar.

"Yes, sir?" the bartender asked as he moved toward Sam.

"I was told I could find a man named Jessup in here," Sam said.

Sam was studying the man's face. From the expression in the his eyes when he heard Jessup's name, the bartender wasn't someone the sheriff could count on as a friend.

"Yeah, he's in here most of the time," the bartender said. "But he left just after lunch. Don't know where he went."

"Too bad. I was hopin' to see him."

"Yeah, well, I expect he'll be back," the bartender said. "Don't reckon we're lucky enough to have somethin' happen to him out on the trail."

"Are you wantin' somethin' to happen to him?" Sam asked.

"Wouldn' cry none," the bartender replied, easily. "No more'n I did this mornin' when Cooper got hisself killed."

"You didn't like Cooper either?"

"Mister, my job ain't to like or to dislike anyone," the bartender growled. "My job is to serve beer and whiskey. Now, you want to drink, or you want to stand here and palaver?"

"I'll have a whiskey."

The bartender made no move.

"Whiskey," Sam said again.

"Heard what you said. Didn't see no money," the bartender replied, flatly.

Sam slapped a quarter on the bar, and the bartender responded by filling a glass.

"You aimin' to put on one of them tin stars?" the bartender asked.

"Seems like the job to have in this town," Sam replied.

"Yeah, don't it?" the bartender replied.

Sam took a swallow. The whiskey was green and bitter, not the worst he ever had, but not far from it. "What do you put in this stuff?" he asked. "Kerosene?"

"I wouldn't waste kerosene in it," the bartender replied, matter-of-factly. He went back to wiping glasses.

"Wait a minute! Wait a minute, hold it here!" someone shouted from behind Sam. When he turned, he saw that the loud-voiced man was sitting at the table where the high-stakes game was being played. "I had a pair of aces up. How'd you know I didn't have them backed up?"

"I didn't know," a powerfully built man across the table answered. "I was just playing a hunch."

"Like hell you was. You knew what my hole card was."

There was a scrape of chairs as the other players began backing away from the table. Sam watched with cool detachment, noticing that all the participants were wearing the tin stars of deputies.

"You ain't sayin' I'm cheatin' or anythin' like that, are you, McCall?"

"No, Muley, it ain't nothin' like that," McCall replied more cautiously. "I . . . I was just admirin' your luck in guessin' when to call, is all."

Sam looked over at the man called Muley. He knew who he was, for he had run across the man's name and description on a few wanted posters. Muley was a bully who got his way by beating up people. That trait made him, perhaps, the least liked of all of Jessup's deputies. On the other hand, one who used his fists as often as Muley was less likely to use his gun. As a result the crimes Muley was wanted for weren't enough to cause anyone to put up much reward money, or to even have his likeness put on the dodgers.

Muley noticed Sam leaning against the bar staring at him, and he looked up. "Want to sit in, mister?" he asked.

Sam set his glass down. "Might do it at that," he replied.

"Come on, then. I reckon your money's as good as anyone's."

CHAPTER 11

SAM AMBLED OVER TO THE TABLE AND pulled out a chair, then dropped three gold double eagles on the table in front of him.

"You ain't one of the local citizens," Muley commented. "Are you?"

"Can't say as I am."

As Muley began to deal, he studied Sam through narrow-slitted eyes. "Do I know you?" Muley asked.

"Don't know if you do or not," Sam replied without elaboration.

"They's somethin' 'bout you that's naggin' at me," he said. He continued to study Sam. "It'll come to me," he said. "It nearly always does."

"I'm sure it will," Sam said easily.

They were playing five-card draw and Sam lost

ten dollars on the first hand, folding cautiously with a hand that was better than the hand Muley was using to run his bluff.

"Ha!" Muley said, pulling in his winnings. "Maybe I should'a warned you. When I play this game, I don't give no quarter."

Sam folded his second hand the same way he had his first, and again Muley, who was the winner, chuckled as he raked in the pot.

When the pot on the third hand reached forty dollars, Sam, who had drawn one card to complete a flush, bet five dollars.

"Better watch yourself there, now," Muley said. "You go to try an' make it all back in one hand, I'm goin' to clean you out good. Want me to show you what I mean? Here's your five and I'm raisin' you five."

Easily, confidently, Muley pushed ten dollars into the pot.

Sam studied his hand, carefully, and once nearly folded. Then, as if he were very unsure of himself, he called.

"All right, mister, let's see what you were holdin'," Muley said, putting down his own jack-high straight.

Sam put down his diamond flush.

"Damn, you had that good a hand an' you just sit there holdin' it like that? You should'a raised instead of called," Muley said. "Ain't you ever played this game before?"

"Sure I've played," Sam said, as if offended by the remark. "I'm doin' all right. I won, didn't I?"

"You won?" Muley snorted. "Mister, you think you're somethin' because you won one lousy pot?"

Sam looked at the pile of money in front of his position. "I got more money now than I started with," he said. "In my book, that makes me better than you." He had been playing to Muley's vanity ever since he sat down, and now it was beginning to pay off. He could see Muley getting piqued at the thought of losing a game to someone as amateurish as he thought Sam was.

"You think you're better'n me, huh?" Muley said. "You sure enough of yourself to up the ante?"

"I don't know if I should," Sam said. "I mean, not with you dealin' the cards."

"You think I'm cheatin', do you?" Muley challenged, angrily.

Sam chuckled. "Not really," he answered. "I reckon if you was cheatin', you'd be winnin'. Right now, you're losin'. But if I'm goin' to bet more, I want to deal."

The others around the table, all of whom had been losing to Muley, laughed, now, at Muley's expense.

Angry, Muley slid the cards across the table. "All right, Mr. Gamblin' Man. You deal."

"Thanks," Sam replied. He picked up the cards and began feeling them as he shuffled. He checked for pinpricks and uneven corners. There didn't appear to be any, which meant that the deck, at least, was honest.

"Now," Muley said, eyeing the money in front of Sam. "What do you say we get to the nut-cuttin'? Let's ante twenty dollars."

Sam pushed twenty dollars into the pot, but the ante was enough to run all but one of the other players away.

Sam dealt the cards and as Muley picked them up, his smile grew broader. "All right," he said. "I'm goin' to open for another twenty bucks."

The third player who had stayed through the ante now groaned, and threw in his cards.

"It's up to you, mister," Muley said. "You goin' to play, or fold?"

"I'll see your twenty," Sam said, sliding the money into the pot. Then he reached into his pocket and pulled out five gold double eagles. "And I'll raise you one hundred."

The easy smile left Muley's face and he stared at Sam, shocked not only by the amount of money Sam had bet, but also by the ease with which he'd bet it. This was not the timid, bungling cowpoke who had been playing.

At first, Muley started to respond to the hundred-dollar bet by raising again. But even as he put his hands on the money he realized it would be a sucker bet. The stranger had set a trap and he'd fallen for it.

The others around the table understood what was going on as quickly as Muley had, and they began to laugh.

"Well now, Muley, what are you going to do next?" one of them asked.

"Yeah, looks to me like he's drawn you in slick as a whistle," another said.

Muley put the money down and stared at the pot. They were right. He had been suckered. It would cost him a hundred dollars now, just to stay, but he couldn't fold, not with three aces and a chance to improve it with the draw. Slowly, he slid one hundred dollars out into the center of the table.

"All right, mister," he growled. "I'll take two cards. And you'd better be particular careful with your deal, 'cause I'm gonna be watchin' you awful close."

Sam's eyes narrowed. "Are you suggestin' I'm cheatin' you?" he asked.

"Ain't makin' no suggestion of the kind," Muley answered. "I'm just tellin' you that I'm goin' to be watchin' pretty close, that's all."

"How many cards?"

"Two," Muley replied.

Sam dealt two cards and Muley groaned, inwardly, when he picked them up. His three aces weren't improved.

"I'll play with what I have," Sam said. "It's still your bet."

"I'll check to the dealer," Muley suggested, knowing even as he spoke that his opponent wasn't going to let that stand.

"Not so easy. It's goin' to cost you another one hundred," Sam said, easily, sliding five more gold coins into the center of the table.

"Mister, how does a a cowpoke like you come by such money?" Muley asked.

"Where the money came from isn't the question," Sam answered. He nodded toward the center of the table. "The question is, Are you goin' to see my bet?"

With an angry snort, Muley threw in his cards. "Three aces!" he said. "What are the chances of losin' when you're holdin' three aces in a two-handed game?"

Carefully, Sam lay his cards on the table, facedown. Then, smiling, he reached for the pot and pulled it toward him.

"Not all that much, I reckon," he said. "But you just got beat."

"Not yet, I ain't beat," Muley growled, reaching down to clamp his hand around Sam's wrist. "Let me see what you got."

Sam looked at Muley, coolly. "Mister, you didn't pay to see what I have," he said.

"Like hell I didn't. I put a hundred and forty dollars into this pot and I say that buys me a look."

Sam held Muley in his gaze for another moment, then he smiled, though the smile never reached his eyes. "All right," he said. "Here's what beat you."

Sam turned his cards over. He had a pair of nines, a jack of spades, a seven of clubs, and a three of diamonds.

"What the hell?" Muley sputtered. "Mister, I don't know who you are, or what you're tryin' to pull. But I don't plan to just sit here an' let you steal a hand from me."

"Don't look to me like he stole it, Muley," one of the other players said. "Looks to me like he won it, fair and square. He called your bluff."

"He ain't gettin' this hand," Muley said. "He didn't even have openers."

"I didn't open," Sam reminded him. "You did." Sam reached for the cards, but before he could get them Muley sent a roundhouse right across the table, connecting squarely with Sam's jaw and dropping him to the floor.

"Well, then," Muley growled. "How's that for openers?" He started to reach for the pot, but Sam jumped up, quickly, sending a whistling left punch which landed squarely on Muley's chin, knocking him away from the table, but not putting him down.

Muley was a man who lived by brute strength, and his strength had just been challenged by someone who was three inches shorter and at least seventy pounds lighter. He smiled at Sam, and Sam was somewhat taken aback. He had hit Muley hard enough to stun a bull, yet Muley hadn't gone down.

"So, you want to play my game, do you?" Muley asked, rubbing his chin. He chuckled. "Well, now, ain't that fine? I reckon Christmas has come early for ole Muley Zorn. Yes, sir, I'm goin' to clean your plow good."

"Mister, you just made yourself one big mistake," one of the other cardplayers said. "Ain't no one ever got the better of Muley."

Sam, being a man of few words, didn't respond

to either comment. Instead, he sent another quick, slashing left into Muley's face. It was a good, well-delivered blow, but Muley just flinched, then laughed a low, evil laugh.

"Fight! They's a fight in the saloon!" someone shouted across the batwing doors, and within a few seconds there were twice as many people in the saloon as there had been when Sam had thrown his first punch.

Sam and Muley circled slowly to their left, studying each other over raised fists, as the crowd in the saloon increased.

"I got five bucks on Muley," someone shouted.

"I got ten on him!"

"I'll take the bets," another said. "I've seen fellas like this one before, skinny and wiry. You ask me, he's tough as rawhide."

Muley, perhaps spurred on by the fact that someone would actually consider betting against him, rushed forward, like a charging bull. Sam stepped nimbly to one side and Muley crashed into the table where they had been playing, smashing it to kindling wood and spilling the money and cards to the floor. With an angry roar, he turned to face Sam a second time.

"Stand still, you chicken-livered bastard!" he shouted.

The crowd continued to urge the two men on, shouting their encourgement to one or the other. Many of them were wearing the badges of authority, yet some of them were rooting for

Sam. That was because even they were often bullied by Jessup's chief deputy.

Muley swung, a clublike swing, which Sam easily avoided. Sam counterpunched and again he scored well. Again, however, Muley merely laughed it off.

A pattern began to emerge as the fight continued. It was obvious that Sam could hit Muley at will, though the punches, individually, had no noticeable effect. However, there was a cumulative effect to the punches, for both of Muley's eyes were beginning to puff up, and there was a nasty cut on his lip. Then Sam caught Muley in the nose with a long left, and when he felt the nose fold up under his hand, he knew that he had broken it. The bridge of Muley's nose exploded like a smashed tomato and started bleeding profusely. The blood ran across Muley's teeth and chin.

Sam began to look for another chance at the nose, but Muley started protecting it. Sam was unable to get to it again, though the fact that Muley was so protective of it told Sam, at least, that the nose was hurting him.

So far, except for the very first, unexpected blow, Muley had not even connected. The big man was throwing great swinging blows toward Sam, barely missing him, but, as yet, Sam was untouched.

After four or five such blows, Sam noticed that Muley was leaving a slight opening for a good right punch, if he could just slip it in across

Muley's shoulder. He timed it, and on Muley's next swing, Sam threw a solid right straight at the place where he thought Muley's nose would be. He hit it perfectly and had the satisfaction of hearing a bellow of pain from Muley for the first time.

Muley was obviously growing more tired now, and he began charging more and swinging less. Sam got set for one of his charges; then, as Muley rushed by with his head down, Sam stepped to one side. Like a matador thrusting his sword into the bull in a killing lunge, Sam sent a powerful right jab to Muley's jaw. Muley went down and out.

For a moment the people in the saloon, who had been noisy partisans during the fight, were stunned into silence. Then from the crowd there came the sound of a solitary person clapping his hands. Sam looked toward the bar to see Charlie Jessup standing there, clapping his hands together, pointedly.

"Well, well, well," Jessup said. "If it isn't my old pal, Sam Slater."

"Slater!" someone gasped.

"The one they call The Regulator?" another asked.

"Slater," another said, and the name was repeated in awestruck tones, throughout the crowd.

"Hello, Jessup," Sam said as he bent down to pick up his winnings from the floor.

"I got word you weren't goin' to come. I heard you turned down the town's offer."

"I did turn down the offer."

"Then what are you doin' here, in Puxico?"

"I figure where I go and when I go is nobody's business but my own," Sam said. He stepped up to the bar and Parmeter handed him a whiskey. When Sam tasted it, it was smooth, much better than the rotgut he had drunk when he first came in. When he looked at the bartender in surprise, the bartender let just the suggestion of a smile play across his lips.

"Normally, I reckon that might be true," Jessup said. "But bein' as I'm the sheriff here, I sort of have a stake in what goes on in my town. Especially if someone is goin' to come into my town and start shootin' and beatin' up all my deputies. That was you shot Cooper this mornin', wasn't it?"

"He never told me his name," Sam said.

Jessup chuckled, dryly. "Well, at least you ain't denyin' it."

"Why should I deny it? I had every right to shoot him. He was about to shoot me."

"Yeah, well, Cooper never was very careful 'bout things like that. So, what are you figurin' on doin' now?"

"I haven't thought much about it."

"How'd you like to throw in with me? I can make you a pretty good offer," Jessup suggested.

"I wasn't interested in the town's offer; what makes you think I'd be interested in yours?"

"'Cause I can offer you a lot more. Besides which, you owe me."

Sam looked at Jessup. "I owe you?"

"Sure. I could'a kilt you the last time we met. Only I didn't."

"No. Instead, you left me for the buzzards."

"You're here."

"Yeah, I'm here," Sam said.

"So, like I say, you owe me. Now, how 'bout throwin' in with me. With the two of us workin' together, we can suck this town dry . . . then go on to another one and start all over again." Muley who was still on the floor but was now coming around, laughed. "Hell, it's better'n robbin' a bank," Jessup added.

"How would you know? You ain't never robbed a bank."

"What makes you think I haven't?"

Sam finished his drink, then wiped his mouth with the back of his hand.

"Because if you had, there would be a big enough reward on you to make it worth my comin' after you," Sam answered. "The way it is now neither you"—Sam looked around at the other deputies, all of whom were now following the conversation from a safe distance—"nor any of these other saddle tramps you have around you are worth a bucket of warm piss."

Sam put his glass down on the bar and started toward the batwing doors. Jessup, watching him leave, grew tempted by the target of Sam's back. Slowly, and unobtrusively, he started to move his right hand toward his pistol.

Even though his back was turned, Sam,

somehow, sensed Jessup's movement. Sam stopped. All he did was stop . . . but that was enough for Jessup. Slowly, Jessup let his gun hand drop back down by his side.

Without turning, or saying a word, Sam walked out of the saloon.

CHAPTER 12

SAM TOOK A ROOM IN THE COMMERCIAL Hotel. He had a bath, then a good dinner in the hotel dining room. Several people noticed him during dinner, and he saw that they were talking about him, but no one came over to talk to him. After dinner, Sam bought a cigar from the hotel tobacconist, then walked outside to take another look at the town.

It was after eight o'clock now, and the sun was a bright red orb, low in the western sky. The fading light was kind to the town, so that the buildings, which had looked bleak and harsh in the noonday sun, were now rimmed with gold and flushed with crimson. A young paperboy, carrying a bundle of one-page news sheets, passed by, hawking his product.

"Paper, mister? Get your paper?"

Sam gave the boy a penny and took one of the papers. *"SEAMUS COOPER KILLED IN SHOOTOUT ON MAIN STREET,"* the headline read over one of the stories. Sam read on.

Yet another shooting has taken place on the streets of what was, once, an industrious and productive town. Seamus Cooper, one of the many deputies illegally appointed by Sheriff Charles Jessup, was shot down in front of the barbershop today by a man identified as Sam Slater.

According to an eyewitness who does not wish to be identified, Sam Slater came into his shop for a haircut and was accosted by Cooper shortly after taking his seat in the barber chair.

"I'll be collecting the tax from you," Cooper is reported to have said.

"What tax would that be?" Mister Slater replied.

"Why, the personal tax, of course," Cooper explained, speaking of that accursed tax which has placed such an unfair burden upon all the good citizens of this beleaguered city.

"Sir, I am but a stranger in your midst and know nothing of this tax," Mister Slater responded.

"Stranger or not, you must pay the tax," Cooper ordered.

"I have no wish to participate," Mister Slater answered.

Upon hearing such an answer, Cooper pulled his pistol and held it within inches of Mister Slater's face. "You shall pay the tax," Cooper ordered, "or I shall sift some lead through you."

Mister Slater is said to have made no reply, nor to have taken any action, until such time as he saw Cooper cock the hammer on the pistol he was holding, a fair indication, if one be needed, that the .44-caliber engine of death was about to be used. Whereupon, our unnamed eyewitness reports, the interior of his tonsorial establishment was filled with the noise of exploding gunpowder. The ball thus energized, however, did not come from Seamus Cooper's .44, but from Sam Slater's pistol, the weapon having been discharged from beneath the barber's apron which had been placed upon Mister Slater's person in preparation for a shave and haircut.

While the death of any human being is a somber event, there are, nevertheless, times when such an occasion is necessary. Legal hangings of desperadoes are one such example. The death of Seamus Cooper is another, for, while not singly responsible for, he was, nevertheless, representative of all that is wrong with our fair town. This writer feels reasonably certain in making the statement that there are none who will mourn his passing.

While it may have been a bullet fired from Sam Slater's pistol which dispatched Seamus Cooper to his appointed rendezvous with the devil himself, in doing so, Sam Slater was but the instrument of justice.

Sam was pleased to see that not everyone in the town of Puxico was content to let Jessup and his deputies run roughshod over them. At least the newspaper editor seemed to have gumption enough to speak out.

Over in the Silver Strike Saloon, however, the reaction to the newspaper article wasn't as positive. Bodine read the story to Payson, Jacobs, and Colby. Afterward, he laid the paper down.

"Well, what do you think of that?" he asked. "This newspaper fella all but said Cooper got what was comin' to him."

"Yeah, well, you got to give it to the little sonofabitch for guts," Payson said.

"And where do you think he got the guts to print somethin' like that? You think he would'a printed this last week? Hell, you think he would'a done it yesterday?"

"Prob'ly not," Payson agreed.

"What you gettin' at, anyway, Bodine?" Jacobs asked.

"I'm thinkin' we're gonna have to do somethin', and we're gonna have to do it quick," Bodine said. "That's my friend lyin' dead up there in Nunlee's Undertaking Parlor. Slater kilt him in cold blood, an' they ain't none of us doin' nothin' about it."

"Truth to tell, I ain't cryin' much over Cooper. He was your friend, he wasn't mine," Colby said.

"Yeah," Jacobs agreed. "You want to do somethin' about it, do it yourself."

"I can't handle Slater all by myself," Bodine admitted. "I don't know, Colby, maybe you can."

"If I go up against Slater, it's goin' to have to be for some reason better'n gettin' even for Cooper," Colby said.

"Yeah, well, how's this for a reason? Jessup wants to get Slater to join in with us."

"Well, hell, what's wrong with that?" Payson asked.

"What's wrong with that? I'll tell you what's wrong with that. If Slater comes in with Jessup, he'll come in at the top. You know what that does to the rest of us? That'll move us all down one notch. Colby, you'll be pickin' shit amongst the chickens with the rest of us, trying to shake down the citizens for personal tax. That'll be less for you . . . and less for us."

"Uh-uh," Colby said. "Ain't no way I'm goin' to get out there with you fellas, chasin' down the citizens."

"Then we're goin' to have to do somethin' about Slater," Bodine insisted.

"If it goes that far, then I'll worry about it,"

Colby said. "In the meantime, leave me out of it."

"Somebody's got to do somethin'," Bodine insisted.

"What can we do?" Payson asked. "Especially if we don't have Colby on our side. Nothin', that's what."

"Maybe we can't do nothin' about Slater yet," Bodine agreed. "But I don't figure to just stand by an' let the rest of the town get ideas from some smart-nosed newspaper man. I think we should pay him a little visit."

"And do what?" Jacobs asked.

Bodine smiled, evilly. "Why, congratulate him on his fine article," he said.

Payson chuckled. "Yeah," he said. "Yeah, I think that might be a good idea."

"Me too," Jacobs threw in.

"How 'bout you, Colby? You with us?" Bodine asked.

Colby shook his head. "Like I told you, Cooper wasn't nothin' to me. You want to do somethin' to the newspaper man, you go right ahead. I got better things to do."

"All right, we'll take care of it ourselves," Bodine said. He laughed. "How hard can it be, anyway? He's just one skinny little newspaper man."

Emboldened by one more drink, the three deputies left the saloon and walked down the street to the office of the *Puxico Vindicator*.

A smallish, balding man, wearing an ink-stained apron, looked up from a platen where he was busy setting type. "Can I help you gentlemen?" he asked.

"You the fella that wrote this here story?" Bodine asked, holding up the single-sheet paper.

"Blanton L. Pipkin, that's me," the newspaper man replied.

"We don't much like what you said," Bodine growled.

Pipkin chuckled. "That's good," he said.

"Good? What do you mean, good?"

"A newspaper that elicits no response from its readers is not doing its job. That fact that you have a response means that my newspaper is an effective organ of the people. Now, do you wish to register a complaint?"

Bodine smiled. "Yeah," he said. "Yeah, a complaint. That's what we want to do."

"Excellent, excellent. Suppose I get you a piece of paper and a pencil? You can sit down right over there and write a letter. I'll print it in the next issue and we can get a real dialogue going."

"Letter? What are you talkin' about? I ain't here to write you no letter."

"I'm afraid I don't understand," Pipkin said. "I thought you said you were here to register a complaint."

"Yeah," Bodine replied. He grinned, evilly. "This kind of complaint."

Bodine pushed over the printing press, then

picked up one of the type boxes and threw it through the window.

"Here! What . . . what are you doing?" Pipkin shouted. "Stop that!"

"Stop that!" Bodine mimicked in a high-pitched, singsong voice. He picked up another box of type and threw it through the space where the window had been. This box, like the first, landed in the street, spilling its type into the dirt. Payson and Jacobs also got into the action so that, soon, the street in front of the newspaper office was littered with type, paper, ink brushes, and other tools of the newspaper trade.

Pipkin ran out into the street and began making a desperate effort to recover his property. By now several other citizens of the town had been drawn to the scene, and they stood around in nervous, uncomfortable silence, watching Pipkin crawl through the dirt.

"Help me, somebody," Pipkin pleaded. "Won't somebody help me?"

Appleby knelt down beside Pipkin and began helping him pick up the scattered type.

"What is the meaning of all this?" he asked.

"Leave it on the ground," Bodine demanded.

"What?"

Bodine drew his pistol and pulled the hammer back. "I said, leave it on the ground," he repeated. "Unless you're aimin' to buy into some of this fella's trouble."

Appleby looked at all the others who had gathered around, imploring them by the expression on his face to join him in this protest. No one responded. Instead, they all looked at the ground, sheepishly.

Sam Slater had been at the far end of the street when he heard the crashing of the window glass. He was just arriving as Appleby stood up, dusting his hands together. Seeing Sam, Appleby smiled.

"Mr. Slater, you'll help, won't you?" he asked.

Sam saw Bodine standing there with his pistol already drawn.

"You plannin' on mixin' in this, Slater?" Bodine asked, menacingly.

Sam shook his head. "Nope," he replied. "This is none of my business."

"Mr. Slater, please!" the newspaper man cried. "Surely you have some appreciation for freedom of the press?"

"The press wasn't free this evenin'," Sam replied, easily. "It cost me a penny."

The others laughed, nervously.

"Yeah," Bodine said. "Can you imagine chargin' a penny for that? I think you ought to give ever'one their money back. And you can start with Mr. Slater here."

Sam held up his hand. "I don't want my money back," he said. "I thought it was well worth the penny. It was a good story."

"Well, now, wait a minute here," Payson said. "Are you for us, or against us?"

"I'm not either one," Sam replied. "Like I said, this is none of my business."

"The way I heard it," Bodine said, "the sheriff was plannin' on fixin' it so's it *was* your business. You are joinin' up with us, aren't you?"

"I have no such plans," Sam said. He started to walk away.

"Is that a fact? Charlie is goin' to be real disappointed to hear that," Bodine said. "He's figurin' on you joinin' us. And the way I look at it, you're either for us, or against us. Now which is it?"

"I'm damn sure not for you," Sam replied. Again, he started to walk away.

"Hold on there, mister!" Bodine barked. "I don't like the way you keep walkin' away from a friendly discussion."

Sam sighed, then turned around. He had made every effort to avoid this, but it was too late now. There was only one way to settle the issue.

"What is your name, mister?"

"The name is Bodine. William T. Bodine. Me and Seamus Cooper was real good friends. Cooper is the name of the man you kilt."

"You're not very careful about choosin' your friends, are you?"

"I heard you shot him through the barber apron. Is that true?"

"I reckon it is."

"I call that a dirty way to kill a man."

"Killin' isn't clean, no matter how you do it,"
Sam replied.

"Cooper never had a chance."

Sam shook his head. "That's right," he said.

"You . . . you admit it!" Bodine sputtered.

"That's right," Sam said. "I admit it. Now,
you say your name is Bodine, is it?"

"Yeah."

"Bodine, I want you to help the newspaper
editor here pick up his type."

There was a collective gasp of surprise from
the onlookers.

Bodine let out a short, ugly laugh.

"You gone loco, Slater? Tellin' me to help
pick up this type?"

"You tell 'im, Bodine," Payson said.

"No, don't tell 'im nothin'. Just gut-shoot the
sonofabitch right there where he's a'standin',"
Jacobs put in.

"I don't plan to tell you again," Sam said.
His words were soft and cajoling, rather than
loud and demanding. And yet, it was that cold,
emotionless softness that made the words
frightening. "Pick up the newspaper man's
type."

"Slater, you got more nerve and less sense
than anyone I ever saw," Bodine said. He moved
the pistol so that it was pointing toward Sam.
"Don't you see that I got the drop on you? All I
got to do is pull the trigger."

Sam shook his head, slowly. "No," he said.
"You may try to pull the trigger, but I'll kill

you before you can get the job done."

Bodine laughed, a nervous little laugh that was as dry as the rattle of bare tree limbs in a hot desert wind. "You'll do what? You may not have noticed it, Slater, but your gun is still in your holster. I could kill you now and no one would fault me for it. In fact, I'd be a hero." He giggled. "I'd be doin' what Jessup and Colby are afraid to do."

"Pick up the type, Bodine, or die with the gun in your hand," Sam said.

The crowd, which had originally been drawn to a noisy altercation, now stood transfixed by the scene that was playing out before them. Like Bodine, they had heard Sam Slater threaten to kill him if he didn't help the newspaper man pick up his type. And like Bodine, they wondered if, perhaps, Sam Slater had lost his senses, for Bodine clearly had the drop on Sam.

"Shoot 'im, Bodine, shoot 'im," Payson said anxiously.

"Yeah, shoot the sonofabitch!" Jacobs added. Though they could no more understand how Bodine might be in danger than could Bodine himself, they couldn't hold back the cold bile of fear that was beginning to well up in each of them.

Bodine forced himself to smile, then started to thumb back the hammer on his pistol. He didn't even get it half-cocked before Sam had his own gun in his hand. There was a snap of primer cap, then a roar of exploding powder, though both events happened so quickly as to be one loud bang. A finger of flame shot from the end of Sam's pistol. Bodine dropped his gun and grabbed his chest. His eyes opened wide in pain and shock. He fell against the doorjamb of the newspaper office, then slid down to the sidewalk, leaving a smear of blood on the wall behind him. He wound up in a sitting position, his eyes open and blank.

"My God, did you see that?" someone in the crowd asked. "Slater just kilt Bodine, while Bodine was holdin' a gun in his hand the whole time."

"I ain't never seen anyone that fast."

Sam looked at the other two deputies. Neither of them had drawn, having felt secure in the fact that Bodine already had his pistol out and in the firing position.

Shooting Bodine had been easy, but only someone with Sam's experience would realize that. Sam had looked deep into Bodine's eyes and knew he would stop and think before he actually pulled the trigger. And, while Bodine was thinking about it, Sam was already doing it. Drawing and shooting, for someone with Sam's speed, was one step . . . not two.

"How about you two fellas helpin' the newspaper man here pick up the type?" Sam ordered.

"Yes, sir," Payson mumbled.

"No! Get away from me! All of you!" the

newspaper man shouted. "I'll pick up my own damn type!"

Sam looked at the newspaper man for a moment, then put his gun in his holster. As he walked away, he could feel the two deputies' eyes boring holes in his neck. He knew they were too afraid to draw.

CHAPTER 13

THERE WERE SEVERAL PEOPLE GATHERED on the street in front of Johnson's Hardware, even though the store was closed now that Ben Johnson and his family had taken the train back to Missouri. However, Nunlee's Undertaking Parlor, which was attached to the rear of the building, was still in business, and it was this fact that had drawn the crowd. Appleby had to pick his way through them in order to go down the side alley to the back entrance of the mortuary.

"Are you goin' inside the funeral parlor, Mr. Appleby?" someone asked.

"Yes, I am."

"Ask 'em how much longer it will be."

"How much longer what will be?" Appleby asked.

"How much longer will it be until they bring the bodies up here and put 'em on display? I hear Sheriff Jessup is goin' to have them laid out in the window of Johnson's Hardware."

"Yes, that's what I heard too," Appleby said.

"So, find out how much longer, will you?"

"I have no intention of satisfyin' your ghoulish curiosity," Appleby growled. "Now, if you will excuse me?"

Once inside the funeral parlor, Appleby saw Doc Sweeny and Lem Miller talking to Abner Nunlee. Nunlee was dressed all in black, as was his custom, and he was wearing a stovepipe hat. Behind him, Appleby could see Bodine's body. It was naked, and Appleby could see the neat, black hole just to the left of center in his chest. On another table lay Cooper's body. Cooper was already dressed in his burial suit. It was dark, with a stiff, white shirtfront and a gray, silk bowtie.

"Abner, you aren't really goin' to display those corpses in the window, are you?" Appleby asked.

"Yes, I am," Nunlee answered.

"But that's macabre! Why would you do such a thing?"

"Because I ain't got no choice in the matter. Sheriff Jessup has ordered it done," Nunlee said. He pointed to two black, lacquered coffins, ornately decorated with silver trim. "And he has chosen two of my finest coffins."

"Did he pay you for them?" Miller asked.

"I reckon you could say that . . . if you figure ten dollars apiece pays for 'em."

"They look more expensive than that."

"Ten dollars is about ten percent of what they are actually worth," Abner replied. He smiled. "I'll tell you this, though. These two august gentlemen may be displayed in these coffins, but they'll never be buried in them. When they go in the ground, they'll be in plain pine boxes."

"Jarred, did you see the sign the sheriff wants to put in the window?" Miller asked, showing Appleby a hand-lettered sign.

**KILLED IN THE STREETS OF PUXICO
BY THE BOUNTY HUNTER SAM SLATER
TWO FINE DEPUTIES
SEAMUS COOPER
WILLIAM T. BODINE**

Appleby sighed, then handed the sign back to Miller. "I have a feelin' there are goin' to be more bodies on display," he said. "Several more."

"Yes, well, as long as it is men like these two, you'll get no complaint from me," Miller said.

"Yes, but it may not be men like these. The next person to die may be an innocent citizen."

"Maybe we made a mistake in contacting Slater," Nunlee suggested. "You never should have gone over there to see him, Doc."

"Now, hold on a minute there, Abner," Doc Sweeny said. "This wasn't my idea. In fact, I was opposed to it. But I seem to recall a donation from you, quick enough, right after the parson got killed."

"I wasn't the only one," Nunlee insisted.

"Anyway, you might have been against it to begin with, but you was the one who went to him with the offer," Miller said.

"So what if I did? He didn't accept our offer," Sweeny pointed out.

"Which, in my mind, makes it all the worse," Miller replied.

"How do you figure that?" Nunlee asked.

"Well, if he was workin' for us, we could call him off now, tell him we don't want him over here anymore. But, bein' as he's here on his own, we got no say in the matter. No say at all."

"At least he's on our side," Appleby suggested.

Miller shook his head. "I wish I could believe that," he said. "But if you ask me, he ain't on nobody's side but his own. You were over at the newspaper office, Jarred, you saw what happened. Why, Slater wasn't even goin' to help Pipkin at all, until Bodine made him mad. What if it had been some citizen who made him mad? Or you? You were there. Suppose Slater had decided to take his wrath out on you? It would be you lyin' naked over there on that table, waitin' for Abner to put the formaldehyde into you."

"What are you suggestin', Lem? That we now ask Slater to leave, the way we asked him to come?"

"It's worth a try."

"No," Doc said. "We'll do no such thing."

"Doc, I figured you'd be the first one to go along with the idea," Miller said. "Seein' as you didn't want him here in the first place."

"You fellas don't know Slater."

"And you do?"

"I think so," Doc said.

"When did you get to be such close friends?"

"I didn't say we were friends, I just said I know him . . . or at least, I know the measure of the man," he added. "Don't forget, he turned down our offer, because he was able to draw the line between bounty huntin' and killin' for hire. I'm not really sure why he is here, now. But I sincerely believe that no one who is innocent has anything to fear from him. I say we just stay out of it. Things have been set in motion now. . . . Let's let it run its course."

"I agree," Appleby said. "Lem?"

Lem nodded. "All right," he said. "I'll go along." He chuckled. "I guess there's really not much else we can do."

When Sam walked by the hardware store a little later, he saw a crowd gathered around the front window. Curious, he went over to see what held their attention. When they saw him coming, they parted like the sea before Moses so that Sam could have an unrestricted view of the ghoulish display of the two corpses.

KILLED IN THE STREETS OF PUXICO
BY THE BOUNTY HUNTER SAM SLATER
TWO FINE DEPUTIES
SEAMUS COOPER
WILLIAM T. BODINE

The bodies of Cooper and Bodine lay side by side. They were, as Jessup had ordered, lying in shiny black coffins which were decorated with ornate silver trim. The hinges were of silver, and at the foot of each coffin there was a spray of silver oak leaves. Just under the viewing glass was a large, spread-winged, silver eagle, and right above the eagle, a silver plate with the name of the deceased inscribed.

The head and shoulders of each of the men were visible through the viewing glass. Seamus Cooper looked as peaceful as if he were sleeping. Bodine, however, wore a vivid mask of death. His eyes had creeped half-open and his upper lip was pulled up, showing his teeth. The edge of his mouth and his cheeks were set in a grimace, as if he were fighting against the pain of the bullet which had struck him.

"Excuse me, Mr. Slater," someone said. "But would you mind standin' just to the left of the window there, so I could get you in this here picture?"

The man who asked the question was setting up a tall, tripod-mounted camera. He draped a black cloth over the camera, then got under it to view the scene through his lens.

"And if you would, hold a pistol across your chest, thusly," the photographer said. "Oh," he said in a sudden burst of enthusiasm. "Do you know what would really look good? If you had two pistols instead of one, and if you crossed your arms across your chest like this." The photographer demonstrated.

"Get someone else for your picture," Sam grunted. He started down the street toward the newspaper office.

Blanton L. Pipkin had managed to get the press back upright and was now tightening the components that had been loosened when it was pushed over. When he heard someone come through the front door he grabbed a crowbar, then stood up and turned around, prepared, if need be, to do battle.

"Take it easy," Sam said, holding out his hands. "I'm not your enemy."

Pipkin lowered the crowbar. "No," he said. "I suppose you aren't."

Sam chuckled. "Were you really goin' to hit me with that thing?"

"If you were bent upon doing further damage to my equipment, the answer is an unequivocable yes," Pipkin responded. He laid the crowbar down, then got back onto his knees and picked up a screwdriver.

"You havin' troubles with it?"

"The tympanum was dislodged," Pipkin said, tightening the hinged wooden cover.

"From the way those men went through here, I'm surrprised there isn't more damage," Sam replied.

"Yes. Well, the Washington handpress is, perhaps, the sturdiest press ever built," Pipkin bragged. "However, even it can be damaged if one sets out to do so."

Finishing his adjustments, Pipkin stood up, moved the tympanum over the bed, then raised it up half a dozen times to test it. Satisfied, he wiped his hands on his apron, then looked at Sam.

"Please forgive me for what might seem to you a lack of appreciation," he said. "I am grateful that your intervention prevented any further damage to myself or my shop. However, the way you did it, by killing Bodine, is the antithesis of all that I stand for."

Sam chuckled. "You do use big words," he said.

"What does 'antithesis' mean?"

"It means 'just the opposite'," Pipkin explained. "Have you ever heard the expression 'throwing out the baby with the bathwater'?"

"Yes."

Pipkin scratched his cheek, and in doing so, left a small ink stain. "That's what I see happening in Puxico," he said. "You see, we are controlled by evil men with violent ways. You, Mr. Slater, have a less evil intent . . . but your ways are just as violent. You have, no doubt, seen the grisly display in the window of Johnson's Hardware?"

"Yes, I've seen it," Sam replied.

"Even though your violence is . . . shall we say, justified, I can't help but wonder what we gain by replacing one form of violence with another."

"You ever seen anyone fight a forest fire?" Sam asked.

"No. You may have noticed, we don't have a great deal of forest country around here."

"I've seen forest fires in the country north of here," Sam said. "Sometimes, the only way to stop one is to start another fire. They call it a backfire." Sam held up his two hands to demonstrate. "The fires burn together . . . then they go out. You lose some . . . but you save much more."

"I see what you mean," Pipkin said. "But what if someone were to be caught between the two fires?"

"He would get burned."

"Precisely, Mr. Slater. And the good citizens of Puxico, it seems to me, are about to be caught between those two fires."

"Not if the good citizens of Puxico are the ones who start the backfire," Sam suggested.

"What do you mean?"

"I mean it's time for Puxico to fight back," Sam said. "If you don't want Jessup as your sheriff, kick him out."

Pipkin shook his head. "It isn't that easy, I'm afraid. We've discussed this very thing before, but we have been unable to come to a consensus as to how best to do it. That is why a few misguided businessmen, with the best of intentions perhaps, but certainly without the unanimous consent of the citizenry, hired you to fight our battle for us."

"Oh, but they didn't hire me," Sam replied. "I didn't accept the offer, remember?"

"Then why are you here?"

"Everyone has to be somewhere," Sam said.

"If you seriously believe that we should fight our own battle, then it would have been better if you hadn't come at all."

"Why?"

"Because the leaders of our fair community will leave it all up to you. Don't you see? Now there is even less of a chance that the town will stand up to Jessup and his gang."

"Oh? How about you? Would you have written that article if I hadn't come to town?"

"I . . . I don't know," Pipkin replied. "Anyway, look what it got me." He took in his office with a wave of his arm. "My press was overturned, my window is broken, and my type is so scattered that it will take me a week to get it straight again."

"Are you sorry you wrote the article, Mr. Pipkin?"

Pipkin stood there for a moment, resting his hand on the press. Finally he looked up at Sam.

"No, by God, I'm not," he answered. "I'm not a bit sorry."

"I was hoping you would say that," Sam said, smiling. "Because there is somethin' I want you to do for me."

"What is that?"

Sam took out a piece of paper and handed it to Pipkin. "I want you to print this," he said.

Pipkin looked at the paper, then read aloud: "Fifty thousand dollars in new greenbacks to go from Commerce to bank in Salcedo. Specie to be transferred by courier on the 17th, instant." Pipkin looked up. "That's tomorrow," he said. "Are you sure you want this printed?"

"Yes, right in the middle of the front page," Sam said.

"But you must know that if Jessup reads this article he's going to go there like flies to honey."

"Yes, that is what I believe," Sam said.

"Then I don't understand. Why would you . . .?" Pipkin stopped in midsentence and smiled. "You want him to go after that money, don't you?"

"I figure that money will get Jessup and some of his gang out of town."

Pipkin scratched his cheek again, leaving yet another smear.

"No, I can't do that," he finally said.

"Why not? Don't you want to get rid of Jessup?"

"Of course I do. But I couldn't do this to the courier . . . set these people on him like that."

"That's the courier's worry, not yours."

"I won't do it to him."

Sam smiled. "Not even if I tell you I'm the courier?"

"You?"

"That's right."

"But you're just setting yourself up as bait. Don't you realize that?"

"If you want to catch a fox, you have to bait the trap," Sam said.

"Maybe that's true. But I've noticed something about bait."

"What's that?"

"Even when you catch the fox . . . the bait is nearly always eaten."

"I might be a little bigger mouthful than the fox can handle," Sam suggested.

Pipkin chuckled. "You know, you might be at that."

CHAPTER 14

AFTER LEAVING THE NEWSPAPER OFFICE, Sam walked two doors down the street, then cut in between two buildings and climbed a set of outside stairs to an upstairs office. This was the office of Doc Sweeny. There was a woman in the doctor's office, and a small boy. The boy's mouth was open, and Doc was holding his tongue down with a wooden depressor as he studied the boy's throat.

"I'll be right with you," Doc said, hearing the jangling bell but not bothering to look around to see who had entered.

The boy's mother looked around to see who had just come in, and, seeing Sam, gasped in quick fear. Sam used to be very self-conscious about this type of reaction, but he was used to it now. The stories that circulated about him were a by-product of his skill and efficiency. Many of the tales of his exploits, including those that demonstrated his fearlessness against over-whelming odds, were true. But there were other stories about him as well, stories that made him into an almost mythological figure, and it was these which tended to frighten women and children.

"How do you do, ma'am?" Sam said, smiling so disarmingly that, for a moment, the woman could almost forget that terrible, disfiguring, purple scar and see him for the handsome young man he could have been. The woman found herself smiling back and feeling a sense of daring, as well as an unbidden, and totally unexpected, sexual excitation.

"I am doing well, thank you, Mr. Slater," the woman said.

"It's nothing but a little congestion," Doc Sweeny told the woman when he finished examin-ing the boy. He handed her a small, brown bottle. "This is a tonic of liverwort syrup and molasses. Give him about a tablespoon of this, three times a day, and the congestion will clear up."

"Thank you, Doctor," the woman said, taking the bottle, then reaching for her son. When she looked at Sam again, the forbidden excitement had, by now, grown so intense that her skin was flushed. "It, uh, was nice to meet you, Mr. Slater," she said huskily, unaware that her secret and developing fantasy could be so easily read.

"The pleasure was all mine," Sam replied.

"Well, I'll be," Doc Sweeny said a moment later, as the woman and her child were using the outside stairs that led down to the street. "I've known Mrs. Thornton for as long as I've been in Puxico and I've never known her to be anything but a fine, decent, upstanding woman. There's not a breath of scandal about her; yet, the way she was just now . . ." Doc let the thought hang.

"Don't make anything out of it, Doc," Sam said easily. He chuckled. "I know *I've* tried a few times in the past, and *I* haven't been able to," he added.

"But the way she was looking at you," Doc said. "It was positively indecent."

"Like you said, Doc, she's a good wife and mother," Sam said. "When somebody like that sees someone like me, she gets a glimpse of the other side of the veil, that's all. You've seen a couple of horses when they've been separated by a fence, haven't you? The black horse has his neck stretched as far as it will go across the fence eatin' grass from the white horse's field, while the white horse has his neck across the fence, eatin' grass from the black horse's field."

Doc laughed. "Now that you bring it up, I suppose I have seen that. I guess, like all adages, 'The grass is always greener on the other side' has a degree of validity. But what brings you up here, Sam? I'm sure you didn't come in here to talk about old sayings."

"No, I didn't," Sam agreed. He walked over to the window in Doc's office and looked out onto the street. From here he had a perfect view of the front of the hardware store, and he could see the two coffins lying there for public viewing. There were still several people standing on the street, looking through the window at the ghoulish display. "Doc, do you want your town back?" he asked.

"Yes," Doc answered, quickly. "But I thought you weren't going to take our offer."

"I'm not," Sam said, turning around.

"Then, I don't understand," Doc said, his face mirroring his confusion. "How are we goin' to get it back?"

"You're goin' to take it back for yourselves," Sam suggested.

Doc laughed, self-deprecatingly. "I don't know," he said. "If you think we can do that, then you have more confidence in us than I."

"I'm going to help," Sam offered.

"Oh, well," Doc said, obviously relieved. "If you're goin' to be here with us then—"

"I'm not goin' to be here," Sam interrupted. "You're goin' to do it alone. I just said I would help."

"I don't understand," Doc said. "How are you goin' to help if you aren't here?"

"I'll explain it to you," Sam said. "But I only want to explain it once. Do you think you can get a few men together? I want good men, men who are dependable, and men you can trust."

"We have a lot of good, dependable, and trustworthy men in Puxico," Doc said. "It's no problem findin' them. But we don't have anyone who knows anything about guns. Why, even the least skilled of Jessup's deputies could take the measure of any of us in a gunfight."

"You let me worry about that," Sam said. "All I want you to do is get them together . . . in secret, if possible."

"We can meet in the upstairs room over Miller's store," Doc suggested, remembering where they'd had met when they'd made the decision to send for Sam in the first place. "Lem Miller is as solid a citizen as we have in this town."

"That's exactly the kind of people we want," Sam said. He looked at the Regulator clock which hung on Doc Sweeny's wall. "Can you have them there by noon?"

"I don't see why not," Doc replied.

When Sam Slater arrived at the Miller General Mercantile Store at noon, he saw that Doc Sweeny had made good on his word. Besides Doc, there were seven others. Sam already knew Appleby, Miller, Pipkin, Nunlee, and Parmeter. Now he was introduced to Jake Suter, the town carpenter, and Ed Alsup, who owned the leather-goods store. Suter was the youngest—Sam guessed he would be about twenty-five, and Appleby, at fifty-five, was the oldest.

"All right, Sam, we're all here," Doc said.

"What do you have in mind?" Nunlee asked.

"Did Doc tell you anything?"

"Doc told us you had an idea we could take our town back," Appleby said.

"That's right. You can take your town back, if you are willin' to make the effort," Sam said.

"We'll make the effort," Suter put in. "You lead us and we'll do whatever you ask."

Sam shook his head.

"I won't be leadin' you," he said. "You are goin' to have to choose your leader from among your own."

"What? Wait a minute," Appleby said. He looked at Doc. "What is this, Doc? I thought you said he was goin' to help us."

"I am goin' to help you," Sam said. "I just won't be leadin' you."

"Then who is goin' to lead us?"

"As I said, you'll have to choose one of your own."

"How do you expect us to do that?" Parmeter asked. "What do we know about guns and killin' and such? We're merchants."

"Yes. Merchants don't fight," one of the others said.

"Is that a fact? Gentlemen, it wasn't all that long ago that more than three million men just like you—farmers, lawyers, doctors, engineers, teamsters, railroaders—men from every occupation under the sun, including merchants," he added, pointedly, "came together to form the mightiest army the world has ever seen. Some of you might remember the War Between the States."

"I damn well remember it," Miller said. "I was in it. I fought at Shiloh with the Fifteenth Ohio."

"How about that? I was at Shiloh too," Parmeter said. He laughed. "Only I was with the Twelfth Mississippi. I reckon it's a good thing we didn't bump into each other then."

"And when you men were at Shiloh, did you do your duty?"

"I didn't skedaddle, if that's what you mean," Parmeter said.

"I reckon I did my part," Miller said.

"Yes, and so did hundreds of thousands of other men just like you. Do you see what I'm gettin' at? You don't need to be fast with a gun or to have a mean streak. Armies are made up of men just like you . . . men with guts and determination. Miller, you and Parmeter have already shown that you have that. Now, what about the rest of you?"

"I figure if a million other men can do it, there's no reason why I can't," Suter said.

"Same here," Alsup replied. "You can count me in."

"Good," Sam replied. "Now, the first thing you have to do is select a leader."

"I figure it should be either Miller or Parmeter," Appleby suggested. "They were both in the war, so they have a little experience in this sort of thing."

"Not me," Parmeter said. "I mean I'll go along

with the rest of you and I'll do my share of the fightin', just like I done at Shiloh. But one thing I learned when I was in the army was that I was a better private than anything else. What about you, Miller? What rank was you?"

"I was a lieutenant by the time the war was over," Miller said.

Parmeter smiled. "Well, then that settles it. Lieutenant Miller of the Yankee army has my vote."

"Any objections from anyone?" Appleby asked. When there were none, he smiled at Miller. "It looks like you're our leader," he said.

"Good," Sam said. "Miller, I want you to plan this like a military battle, because that's exactly what it's goin' to be. Get your men together, figure out a plan of attack, then attack. And I figure the best time to do it is tomorrow."

"Tomorrow?" Miller replied. "No, that's too soon. We've got to have a few meetings, work out some—"

"No time for all that," Sam interrupted. "It has to be tomorrow."

"Why tomorrow?"

Pipkin smiled broadly. "I believe I know why it must be done tomorrow," he said. "It's because tomorrow, Jessup will be gone."

"Gone? Gone where?" Appleby asked.

"Well, if I were a bettin' man, I would say he is going to be waiting somewhere on the road to Salcedo," Pipkin said. When it was obvious that no one else knew what he was talking about,

Pipkin told them about the article he was printing, stating that fifty thousand dollars in new greenbacks was being transported by courier to the bank in Salcedo.

"Fifty thousand dollars?" Alsup said. He let out a low whistle. "That's more money than there is in the whole world."

Sam chuckled. "It's not more money than there is in the whole world," he said. "But it is a lot of money. I had to make it a lot of money in order to tempt Jessup. But, since the courier isn't goin' to be carryin' any money at all . . . it's as easy to say he's carryin' fifty thousand as it is to say he's only carrying ten thousand."

"What are you talkin' about?" Parmeter asked.

Miller smiled, broadly. "I think I know," he said. "You are goin' to be the courier, aren't you, Sam?"

Sam nodded.

"That's pretty good," Miller said. "Yes, sir, that is pretty damn good."

"What's pretty good?" Suter asked. "What are you talkin' about?"

"Don't you see, boys? As soon as Jessup reads that newspaper article, he's goin' to hightail it after that money shipment. Only, there is no money. Slater here is actin' as a decoy for us. He's goin' to draw Jessup out of town."

"Not only Jessup," Sam said. "Unless I miss my guess, he'll want two others with him. Any more and the split will be too little, any less and he·can't be sure he can get the job done."

"Which leaves the others for us," Miller concluded.

"Think you can handle them?" Sam asked.

"I think we'll be ready," Miller said. "What do you boys think?"

Pipkin smiled. "I say, give us our marchin' orders, Captain. The Puxico Volunteer Militia is ready to go to war."

"Charlie, you seen this?" Payson asked, dropping the paper on Jessup's table.

Jessup, who was playing a game of solitaire, glanced up.

"What is it?" he grunted. "Another editorial from our fearless newspaper man?"

"Uh-uh, nothing like that," Payson said. "Read this here story." Payson pointed to an article on the front page.

Jessup glanced at it, and then, when his interest was aroused, picked it up and began reading it. Not until he was finished with the article did he make a comment.

"Have you talked to anyone about this?" he asked.

"Not yet. I figured I would show it to you first."

"Good, good," Jessup said. He looked around the saloon and saw nearly half a dozen of his deputies in various pursuits . . . drinking, playing cards, or talking with the girls. He knew that at least two others, including Colby, had gone upstairs with a girl. "Get Muley and the two of you come upstairs to my room. Don't let anyone know what's goin' on."

"What about Colby?"

"Especially not Colby," Jessup said.

"All right," Payson replied. "I'll get 'im, and we'll be right there."

Jessup closed up the deck, then left his table and walked up the stairs to the second-floor landing.

"Charlie, you want to sit in here?" one of the deputies called.

Jessup yawned and stretched. "No, I think I'll get a little shut-eye," he answered. "Maybe later."

Once in his room, he rolled himself a cigarette, then waited until Muley and Payson showed up. They came in a few minutes later.

"Did anyone see you come up?" Jessup asked.

"No," Payson replied.

"Anyway, what difference would it make?" Muley asked. "These are our boys."

Jessup smiled, then shook his head. "Not for this, they ain't," he said.

"Not for what? What's goin' on, Charlie? All Payson said was that you wanted to see us."

"Muley, how would like to have ten thousand dollars?" Jessup asked.

"Ten thousand dollars? Where would I get that kind of money?"

"I'm goin' to give it to you," Jessup said.

Muley laughed, then frowned. "You got that kind of money, Charlie?" he asked.

"Not yet," Jessup admitted. "But after the three of us pull a little job, I will have. There's goin' to be ten thousand apiece for each of you."

"Wait until I tell the others," Muley said, smiling broadly.

"No!" Jessup said, quickly. "That's exactly what you aren't goin' to do. This one is just for us."

"How are we goin' to keep Colby from findin' out?" Muley asked. "Seems like that sonofabitch knows ever'thing that goes on."

Jessup thought of Colby's taunting him over his trouble with women.

"Yeah," Jessup said. "Sometimes it does seem that way. So we'll just have to make certain that he doesn't find out, that's all. Payson, you go around and gather up all the newspapers so he doesn't learn about the money shipment. And both of you, make certain you don't say one word about this."

"You can count on me, Charlie. I ain't sayin' nothing," Muley promised.

"Me neither," Payson added.

"All right, that takes care of that," Jessup said. "Now, according to the newspaper article, the money is being transferred from Commerce to Salcedo. That means the courier is going to have to pass through Fiddler's Draw. When he gets there, we'll be waiting for him. But, if we're goin' to get there on time, we're goin' to have to get an early start, so we're goin' to slip out one at a time, early in the mornin'. We'll meet about three miles out of town." Jessup held up his finger. "And if either one of you aren't there, I'll go on without you. Think about that. If you sleep late, you'll be costin' yourself ten thousand dollars."

"I'll be there," Muley promised.

"Me too," Payson added.

CHAPTER 15

BOB PAYSON LEFT FIRST, RIDING OUT OF Puxico at about six A.M. the next morning. Muley left around eight, and Jessup at about eight-thirty. Parmeter watched them all leave. Had Parmeter not been at the citizens' meeting the day before, he would have been as much in the dark as Rufus Colby and the dozen or so deputies who remained behind.

As soon as Jessup left, however, Parmeter hurried down to the mercantile store to give Miller the news.

"All right," Miller said with a look of grim determination on his face. "This is what we've been waiting for." Miller looked over at the clock on his wall. "Parmeter, you pass the word to all the deputies that Jessup wants a meeting with

SLAUGHTER ✪ AT PUXICO

them in your saloon at ten o'clock. We must
have all of them in there then. And also—this is
important—make sure that no one else except
the deputies are in the saloon."

"What about the whores?" Parmeter said.
"They'll still be asleep at ten."

"I don't know. I hate leavin' them in there,
but if they all leave it could cause someone to
get suspicious."

"Actually, I think I can sneak the girls out
the back way," Parmeter said. "But it's the
other customers I'm worried about. I sure can't
take them through the back without arousing
suspiscion.

Miller stroked his chin for a moment. "Yeah,"
he said, "I see what you mean." Suddenly he
smiled. "Say, I've got an idea. Why don't you
have the deputies run the customers out for
you?"

"How? What do you mean?"

"It's simple. You just post a sign that reads,
'By order of Sheriff Jessup, the saloon is closed
to all citizens today.' If the deputies think that's
what Jessup wants, they'll do it for you."

Parmeter laughed. "Yeah," he said. "Yes, I
believe that would do it."

"I'll get all the others together. We'll meet in
Johnson's Hardware. You come down and join
us as soon as you can get away. And Parmeter?"

"Yeah?" Parmeter asked, looking back.

"Be armed," Miller said.

Parmeter smiled. "You're damn right I will

be," he said. "I've been waitin' on this a long time."

Miller watched Parmeter leave, then went to the back of the store, into the area of the building which served as the living quarters for himself, his wife, and his two children. He dragged an old trunk out from beneath the bed. Opening the lid, he began going through all the items which had, long ago, been so carefully packed inside. There was the dress Nonnie had worn when they were married . . . the christening gown worn by both children at their baptisms . . . a wool shawl passed down from his grandmother and said to have been made by some ancient relative in the old country. Finally he found what he was looking for.

"Lem?" a woman's voice called softly.

Miller turned around to see his wife standing in the doorway. "Lem, what is it?" she asked. "Why are you looking around in the trunk?"

"What are you doin' back here, Nonnie? One of us has to watch the store."

"Never you mind the store, Lem Miller," his wife said. "Something is going on and I want to know what it is. You had that mysterious meeting yesterday, Mr. Parmeter was just over here, and now you're going out again." She saw what he was holding in his hand. "What are you doing? That's your old army uniform, isn't it?"

"Yes, it is," Lem said. He sniffed it, and it smelled of cedar and mothballs. He held up the light blue pants and the dark blue jacket. On its shoulders were the red shoulder boards of an artillery lieutenant. "I wonder if I can still get into it." He stripped off his shirt, then stuck his arms into the sleeves of the jacket.

"Lem Miller, I want to know what is going on," his wife insisted.

Miller smiled when he found that he could still get the jacket buttoned. "Look at this, Nonnie," he said. "It's a perfect fit."

Miller's wife began to sob, quietly. When Miller saw her, he went over and put his arms around her. "What's wrong?" he asked.

"That's what I want to know," she replied. "Lem, Lem, you are frightening me. I asked you what is going on and you won't tell me."

Miller sighed. "All right, Nonnie, I'll tell you, but you must promise to say nothing about it, do you understand? Say nothing to no one, for if you do speak about it, you could put several people's lives in danger . . . including mine."

"Lem, you are making me even more frightened," she said. "What have you done?"

"It's not what I have done," Miller replied. "It's what I am goin' to do . . . or rather, what *we* are goin' to do. We're takin' back our town."

"Taking back our town? What do you mean? And who is 'we'?"

"Appleby, Parmeter, Doc Sweeney, a few others, and me," Miller said. "Nonnie, we're goin' to run Jessup and those rascal deputies out."

"Lem, no," his wife pleaded. "Let someone else

worry about that. You're not a lawman . . . you're a store clerk."

Miller looked hard at his wife. "Woman," he said. "I served very proudly under a store clerk at Shiloh. His name was U. S. Grant, and when he was needed, he answered the call. Now, give me your prayers or your silence . . . but stay out of my way!"

Nonnie put her arms around him. "I'm frightened," she said.

"That's understandable," Miller replied. "Anytime a man goes off to war, he leaves behind a family who is frightened for him. But that doesn't stop him from doin' his duty. You remember how it was."

"That was different. We were both very young then, and there were no children."

"Believe me, Nonnie, life was just as precious then as it is now," Miller said. He brushed a fall of hair back from her forehead and kissed her there. "Don't be frightened," he said. "This is somethin' that must be done."

Nonnie took a deep breath, then nodded. "I know it is," she finally said. "And I'm very proud of you for doing it. But that doesn't stop me from being afraid."

Miller picked up a bow and a quiver of arrows.

"Oh, Lem, you aren't going to try and fight those gunmen with a bow and arrow?" Nonnie asked, aghast.

Miller smiled. "That's exactly what I'm goin' to do," he said.

"But why? I don't understand."

"I know you don't," Miller replied. "I hope they don't either. Now, don't be frightened for me, do you hear? I'll come back to you without a scratch. I promise you." He put on his campaign hat, and then, carrying his bow and the quiver of arrows, went out through the back door so he could go to Johnson's Hardware by way of the alley.

Over in the Silver Strike Saloon, Colby was still asleep when one of the girls knocked on his door and began calling quietly for Linda Sue. Linda Sue had spent the night in Colby's bed and was now lying beside him, snoring softly. Though she was the one being called, Colby was the one who was awakened.

"What do you want?" Colby called.

"Mr. Colby, I need to see Linda Sue. Would you send her out, please?"

"Yeah, yeah, take her," Colby grumbled. He pushed on Linda Sue's shoulder. Of all the girls in the place, she was always the hardest to wake up. "Get up, woman," he said.

Linda Sue woke up. "What is it?" she asked.

"I don't know, somebody wants you out there."

"Umm, and I was sleepin' so good. Tell her to come back."

"You were snorin' like a hog," Colby growled. "Get on out there and see what she wants. Maybe that way I can get a little rest."

"Do you want me to come back, sweetie?"

"No," Colby growled. He liked having a woman at night, but he didn't care that much for them the next morning. "Be gone with you."

Linda Sue slipped into her clothes, quickly, then stepped out of the room. Colby heard them whispering about something outside, and put the pillow over his head to block them out. Whatever they had to say couldn't possibly be important enough to interrupt his sleep.

Colby did manage to go back to sleep, though it didn't last long, for sometime later there was a loud, impatient knocking on the door, followed by a man's gruff voice.

"Colby! Colby, are you asleep?" an insistent voice called.

"Who the hell can sleep with all this bangin' and yellin'?" Colby replied, irritably.

Colby got out of bed and walked over to the door. When he jerked it open he saw Jacobs standing there.

"Damnit all to hell, Jacobs, what's goin' on around here this mornin'?" he asked. "First the damn women wake me up, and now you. What do you want?"

"Jessup has called a meeting for ever'body at ten o'clock," Jacobs said. "It's pert' near that now."

"A meetin'? I didn't hear anythin' about a meetin'. What's it about?"

"I don't know," Jacobs said. "But it must be important. I've never known him to call any meetings before."

Colby ran a hand through his tousled hair, then scratched his chin. "All right," he said. "All right, tell 'im to hold his horses. I'll be down there in a few minutes."

Colby poured some water from the pitcher into the basin and splashed some of it onto his face. Then he got dressed, pulled on his boots, and strapped on his gun.

As Colby reached for his hat, he happened to look out through the window. His room was upstairs and in the back of the saloon, so the window didn't open onto the street, but, through the alley opening, he could see some of the street, and what he saw puzzled him. He saw Suter and Appleby going into the closed hardware store. Seeing two of the local businessmen going into a closed store wasn't, in itself, curious. But both Appleby and Suter were carrying rifles . . . and Colby did find that mildly curious.

Putting that aside, he finally went downstairs, where he saw all the deputies sitting around the tables, talking quietly among themselves. He noticed, with some irritation, that neither Jessup nor Muley were here. If Jessup wanted to call a meeting, Colby thought, the least he could do would be to show up.

Colby walked over to the bar, then looked up and down for the barkeep.

"Parmeter," he called. "Parmeter, you back there?"

"Parmeter ain't here," one of the deputies said.

Colby turned his back to the bar. "Where is he?" he asked.

"I don't know."

Colby looked around the saloon. It was exceptionally quiet, and except for the deputies, no one else was here. There was something not quite right about things, and Colby scratched his chin.

"What is this?" he asked. "What's goin' on?"

"I don't know," Jacobs answered. "All I know is, we got word that Jessup wanted a meeting with all of us, an' he posted that sign over there tellin' ever'one else to stay away."

"There's somethin' . . ." Colby started to say, but he was so unable to put his finger on what was bothering him that he couldn't even form the words to express his concern. As a result, he let the sentence dangle, uncompleted.

"What?" Jacobs asked, totally unaware of anything untoward about the situation.

"Nothing," Colby said. "I need a drink, that's all." With Parmeter absent, Colby walked around behind the bar to pour his own liquor. He stood back there for a moment while he tossed half of his drink down.

"All right, we're here," he said. "So where the hell is Jessup?"

"I don't know, he ain't showed up yet."

"What about Muley? Don't he have to make the meeting?" Colby asked.

"He ain't here either."

"Neither is Payson," one of the other deputies

replied. "I went to get him over to the livery. . . .
Payson has a room there, but he wasn't nowhere
around."

"Jacobs, go up and knock on Jessup's door,"
Colby said.

"Not me," Jacobs replied. "Jessup don't like
being woke up early in the morning."

"I said go up and knock on his door," Colby
said again, his words cold and demanding.

"All right, all right, you don't have to get
into a huff over it," Jacobs said, holding up
his hands as if warding Colby off. "I'll do it,
but I'm goin' to tell him it was you made me
do it."

Colby walked over to the batwing doors and
looked out onto the street. He didn't see anyone
. . . not one wagon, horse, or pedestrian. He
looked toward Johnson's Hardware, but saw
nothing there either. Finally he tossed down the
rest of his drink, then walked back to the bar to
pour himself another one.

"What day is today?" he asked. "Is this
Sunday?"

"Sunday? No, it's Thursday, I think. Or maybe
Friday," someone answered. "Why?"

"I don't know," Colby said. "It just seems
awful quiet to me for some reason."

Jacobs came back down the stairs.

"When's he comin' down?" Colby asked.

"I don't know."

"What do you mean, you don't know? Didn't
you ask him?"

"I couldn't ask him, Colby. There weren't no one in his room. There ain't no one in Muley's room, neither."

"What the hell is goin' on around here?" Colby asked. He moved quickly up the stairs to Jessup's room. "Jessup?" he called. "Jessup, you up here?"

He pushed open the door to Jessup's room and saw that, as Jacobs had said, it was empty. Then he smiled. Jessup was probably with one of the women, and with his "problem," Colby thought to himself, he was probably having a hard time of it. "Or maybe, it's not so hard," he said out loud. "Yeah, maybe that's the problem." He laughed aloud at his own joke.

"Jessup, are you down there with one of the women?" he called, walking down toward the end of the hall where the five women had their rooms. He knocked on the first woman's door, and when he got no answer, he pushed it open. Like Jessup's room, this one was empty.

"Linda Sue?" Colby called. He knew Linda Sue was here . . . she'd just left his room a short time ago. "Linda Sue, where the hell are you?"

Colby pushed open the door to Linda Sue's room, but she was gone too. So was Annie, and so were all the other girls. The entire top floor was empty.

"What the hell is goin' on here?" Colby muttered again. He started to go back out into the hallway, but, just as he did, something outside the window got his attention. He thought he had seen someone moving on the roof of the leather-goods store across the street.

"You're a dumb sonofabitch to be patchin' your roof in the heat of the day," he said, moving over to the window for another look.

At first, there was no one there, and he started to turn away. But then he saw another movement on the roof of the apothecary.

"What the hell? Are two of you patchin' your roof?" he asked. He stayed by the window for a long moment, continuing to look outside, then saw one of them move again. This time he got a very good look at him. The man on the roof was Alsup, and he wasn't carrying patching material. Like Appleby and Suter before him, he was carrying a rifle. Suddenly it all came together and Colby knew what was going on.

"Son . . . of . . . a . . . bitch!" he said aloud. He darted out of the room and bolted down the stairs. "Get your guns!" he shouted. "Get your guns! We're about to be attacked!"

CHAPTER 16

"WHAT ARE YOU TALKING ABOUT, ATTACK?" Jacobs asked. "Who's attacking us? Indians?" he laughed.

"No, goddamnit, the town is," Colby said. "Hell, half the damn town is crawlin' around out there on roofs and behind the buildings. And they've all got rifles."

Jacobs walked over to the batwing doors to look outside. At that precise moment he saw someone with a rifle looking out one of the upstairs hotel rooms.

"Sonofabitch! He's right!" Jacobs yelled. He drew his pistol and shot toward the hotel. His bullet punched a hole in the glass window, but other than that, it did no damage.

"What did you shoot for, you dumb bastard?" Colby shouted.

"What are you talking about? I seen someone in the hotel window with a rifle pointed toward us," Jacobs answered.

"As long as they thought they had us in the dark, we had the advantage," Colby said. "Now they know that we know."

"So what? There ain't nothing out there but a bunch of ribbon clerks and storekeeps," Jacobs replied. "Why don't we just go out there and . . . unnh!"

Jacobs's sentence was cut short by a bullet fired from a rifle from somewhere across the street. The bullet caught him high in the chest and spun him around. Spewing out a little fountain of blood, he put his hand up to the wound to stanch the flow, but the blood streamed through his fingers. He looked up with an expression of surprise on his face.

"A ribbon clerk," he said. "Who would've thought?"

"Get these tables turned over, men," Colby shouted. "Get 'em up to the windows! We've got a fight on our hands!"

Lem Miller was climbing up onto the roof of the hardware store when he heard the shooting start. He hurried to get there, but as he was carrying the bow and arrows, and a heavy box, his movement was somewhat restricted. He was a little aggravated because the shooting wasn't supposed to start until he gave the command, and as soon as he got onto the roof he mentioned it.

"We couldn't help it, Lem," Appleby replied. "They must've seen us. They started the shootin'."

"All right, it doesn't matter," Miller said. "The ball is opened now. It's up to us to give them all they can handle. Help me with these, will you?"

"Sure, Lem. What do you want me to do?"

Miller opened the lid of the case he was carrying, revealing the contents. It was an entire case of dynamite sticks.

"Start tyin' them onto the arrows," he said. "About here." He indicated where the sticks should go.

For the next few minutes, bullets flew overhead as Miller and Appleby worked to tie the dynamite sticks to the arrows. When they had about ten of them done, Miller lit a cigar, then handed it to Appleby.

"You light them," he said. "I'll shoot them."

Smiling, Appleby held the hot end of the cigar to the dynamite fuse. "Consolidated Mining never saw its dynamite put to a better use," he said.

When the fuse was sputtering, Miller raised up and shot the arrow toward the front of the saloon. It fell short, landing in the water trough just in front. A moment later the dynamite went off, splintering the trough and throwing up a shower of water.

"I didn't compensate enough for the weight

of the dynamite stick," Miller said, picking up a second arrow. "I'll put this one inside."

With the second fuse sputtering, Miller raised up to loose another arrow. A fine stream of smoke marked the path of the arrow from the roof of the hardware store, across the street, then through the front window of the saloon, right between the letter r on Silver and the letter S in Strike. A moment later there was an explosion inside the the saloon which blew out the windows and sent the batwing doors flying out into the street.

Four deputies came outside then, firing as they ran. They were cut down by a hail of bullets from the citizen army.

"Cease-fire!" Miller shouted. "Cease-fire!"

The firing stopped and for a moment there was absolute silence. Then, as the members of the citizen army realized they had won, they began to cheer.

Doc Sweeny was the first one to go down onto the street, where, once again the doctor, he began examining the bodies to see if anyone was left alive. The others joined him in the street, laughing and talking about their victory, happy and proud that, once again, the town belonged to them.

"I'd better check inside the saloon," Doc said. "There may be some wounded in there."

"I'm goin' to go back up and get the dynamite off the roof," Miller said. "If it stays out in the sun and gets too hot, it might go off."

"Yeah, we don't want to destroy another building," Parmeter laughed. "I'm goin' to need all of you to help me rebuild mine."

Miller, feeling a sense of pride, accomplishment, and relief that he had not felt the day the war ended, climbed back onto the roof of the hardware store. He had just closed the lid of the box holding the dynamite when he heard the sound of a pistol shot. Startled, he hurried over to the edge of the roof to see what had happened.

Doc Sweeny came out of the saloon, walked out into the middle of the street, then collapsed.

"Someone shot the doc!" somebody yelled.

Miller wondered who could have done it. He thought everyone was dead. The mystery was solved when he saw Rufus Colby come out of the saloon, apparently unhurt by the blast that had gone off inside. Colby was holding a pistol in his hand, which gave him an advantage over every member of the citizen army. Most of them had left their rifles behind, thinking the battle was over. Suter and Nunlee had their rifles with them, but they were holding them loosely by their sides.

"Well now," Colby said. "You fellas had yourself quite a little party here, didn't you? Well, the party is over. But you've left me with a little problem. There are five of you and I have only four bullets left. Who will I kill and who will I spare?" He smiled, evilly.

"I know. I'll spare the undertaker. After all,

someone will have to bury the dead." He pointed his pistol at Appleby. "You first, Appleby. I'm sure you are the one who organized this little get-together."

Colby pulled the hammer back on his pistol and aimed carefully at Appleby. Appleby began shaking, but he didn't say a word. For a moment there was an eerie tableau vivant, with everyone paying such close attention to the drama being performed that no one saw the little plume of smoke zip down from the roof across the street. Not until the arrow buried itself in Colby's chest did they become aware of what had just happened.

"Get down!" Miller shouted from the roof.

Colby clutched at the arrow in his chest, attempting to pull it out. Then he suddenly realized that his troubles were much more serious than just the arrow itself, for tied to the arrow was a stick of dynamite, its fuse sputtering.

Colby's eyes grew wide in recognition and horror.

"No!" he shouted.

The others dived for the ground just as the stick of dynamite went off.

Sam had been aware that three men were dogging him, riding parallel with him. Actually, he knew this more from some extra sense than from any direct observation, for the men trailing him were so good at their job that he had not yet seen them.

He also knew when they left him, riding ahead of him in order to get into position to set up the ambush, even though he did not see them leave, any more than he had seen them when they were following.

Sam didn't need to see them to know they were there and he didn't need to see them to know who they were. He knew that it was Jessup and whoever Jessup had decided to bring along with him.

Several times during the ride Sam had stopped and lifted his canteen from the pommel to take a drink of water. Each time he stopped he would shove the cork back, then rehang his canteen. After that he would wipe the back of his hand across his mouth and stand in the stirrups to look around nervously. Each of these carefully staged episodes would conclude with him sitting back down and patting the bulging saddlebags.

All this was for the benefit of his shadows. While he actually did look around each time, he was really only pretending to be nervous. And the patting of the bulging saddlebags was strictly for effect. He wanted Jessup to believe that fifty thousand dollars in greenbacks were being transported, just as the newspaper article had stated. In fact, there was no money at all. From the planted newspaper article to the feigned nervousness on the trail, it was all a ruse.

One of the reasons Sam had chosen this

particular route was because there was only one obvious place for an ambush. The thing about ambushes, however, was the fact that they only worked when they were a complete surprise. If the ambushers were themselves surprised, then the whole thing could be turned around. And that was exactly what Sam planned to do.

The ambush point was just ahead, where the trail squeezed down to a narrow path going through a needle-like draw. At the other end of the draw a real courier would be a sitting duck. Since Jessup and whoever was with him had gone on ahead of Sam some time ago, Sam knew that they were waiting for him now.

When Sam reached the draw he knew that for the next several seconds he would be out of the line of sight of those who were waiting for him. This, then, was where he would have to make his move. As he passed under a large rock outcropping, he stood in his saddle, found a good handgrip, then pulled himself up into the rocks. Once in the rocks, he was able to climb over the top of the pass while his horse continued on through.

He ran at a crouch to the far end of the pass. From there, he could hear the slow, measured clop of his horse's hooves echoing through the long, narrow canyon. He pulled his pistol and waited . . . just as he knew Jessup was doing.

The sound of the hoofbeats came closer until they were almost upon him.

"Now!" somebody suddenly shouted, and

the narrow chasm was filled with the sound of exploding gunshots and whistling bullets.

Sam's horse, riderless of course, bolted out of the canyon.

"Grab the horse!" Jessup shouted. "The money's in the saddlebags!"

Muley stepped in front of the horse and threw his arms up. The horse slid to a stop, its iron hooves striking sparks on the rocky ground. It reared defiantly, but Muley's action had effectively stopped its bolt.

Muley grabbed the halter and the horse grew calm.

"All right, hold him, hold him!" Jessup shouted.

Sam had not yet been seen by the outlaws, so he was able to observe everything without himself being observed. He saw now that the third man in the little group was Bob Payson.

"Hey! Where's the courier?" Payson asked.

"We must've hit him," Jessup said. "He's prob'ly lyin' back there on the trail."

"Let the sonofabitch lie there," Muley said. "We've got the money, that's all we need."

"No," Jessup said. "I left a man once before and he didn't die. This time I aim to finish the job."

"I'm glad to see that you are a man who learns from his mistakes, Jessup," Sam said, suddenly standing up.

"Damn! It's Slater!" Payson said, raising his pistol.

Sam dropped Payson with one well-placed

shot. Muley, thinking that Sam was preoccupied with Payson, tried to take advantage of the fact. The shot which dropped Muley was so close on the heels of the first that the two sounded almost as one. When Sam looked toward Jessup, he saw that the outlaw had both hands up in the air.

"I ain't makin' no fight of it, Slater," Jessup said. "Do you see? I've got my hands straight up in the air. I ain't makin' no fight of it."

It was early evening, though not yet dark, when Sam led the little party back into Puxico. Jessup, looking sullen, was bound hands and feet in his saddle. Muley and Payson, both dead, were belly-down across theirs. Sam noticed the difference in the town, even before he saw the damaged saloon. There were people on the street, more people than he had ever seen on the streets of Puxico before. And they were laughing and animated. As he passed by Johnson's Hardware he saw why. There, in the front window, not in coffins but tied to boards, were the bodies of seven deputies. When Sam pulled up in front of the sheriff's office, he was met by Miller and Appleby.

"Looks like a few changes have been made," Sam said as he swung down from the saddle.

"I'd say a few," Appleby said. He saw Jessup sitting there, then the two bodies. "And with these galoots, it's complete," he added.

"I didn't see Colby."

Appleby laughed. "And you won't," he said. "There's not enough left of him to see."

Sam looked over toward the saloon. "It does sort of look like you called out your artillery."

"What are we going to do with Jessup?" Appleby asked.

"Why, hell, we're goin' to hang him," Sam said, easily.

"Hang him?"

"That's what generally happens to the people I bring in," he said.

"Sam, we can't hang him," Miller said.

"Are you getting squeamish on me?" Sam asked.

"Squeamish? No, it ain't that," Miller said. He stroked his chin. "It's just that . . . well, we took our town back from Jessup because he was lawless. I don't want to see us become the same thing, and hangin' him now without a trial would be nothing more than a lynchin'."

Sam nodded toward the hardware store. "You got seven bodies lying in the front window back there, don't you? Did you have a trial for them?"

"No, but that was different. We were the same as at war with them."

"Nobody ever gets hung during a war?"

"Sure—spies, murderers, and the like," Miller said.

"All right, there's your legal justification," Sam said. "The town of Puxico raised a militia and elected you its commander. Until all the trouble is over, I'd say Puxico was under martial law, wouldn't you?"

"I don't know," Miller mused.

"Lem, I think a very good case could be made for that," Appleby interjected. "We damn well better be able to—otherwise even the killing of the deputies isn't legal."

"All right," Miller said. "I suppose we were under martial law."

"*Are* under martial law," Sam corrected. "Martial law won't be lifted until it's all over with, and it won't all be over with until Jessup is tried. As the commander, all you have to do is convene a court, select a jury, and appoint a prosecutor and counselor for the defense."

Jessup's face grew as gray as dust. "You can't do this to me," he said. "You got no right to do somethin' like this."

"On the contrary, sir," Blanton L. Pipkin spoke up. He had been standing to the side, listening to the entire conversation. "You see, you, yourself, have already established the precedence of a court in this town. With martial law in effect, the commander of the militia, in this case Lem Miller, has every right and legal justification to utilize the court thus established to carry out the edicts of his military government. I have no doubt but that any decision such a court makes would be upheld . . . all the way up to and including the Supreme Court of the United States."

"Mr. Pipkin," Miller said. "Would you act as prosecutor in this case?"

"I would be pleased to do so," Pipkin said.

"And you, Jessup," Miller said, "may choose as your defense attorney, anyone you want."

"Ha! A fat choice I have," Jessup said. He looked into the faces of all the men gathered there in front of the sheriff's office, then suddenly broke out in a broad, evil smile. "All right. I choose Sam Slater."

"Slater can't defend you," Miller said. "He knows damn well you are guilty."

"That doesn't matter," Pipkin spoke up. "It isn't necessary that a defense lawyer believe his client is innocent. It is only necessary that the lawyer provide the best defense possible under the circumstances."

"Mr. Slater, would you defend this man to the best of your ability?" Miller asked.

Sam looked at Jessup for a long moment before he answered. "Yeah," he finally said. "I will."

"All right, gentlemen," Miller said. "Pipkin will prosecute, Slater will defend, and I will act as judge. Court will convene at Johnson's Hardware in one hour."

Though the trial began just a little over an hour later, the entire town had gotten word of it, so that nearly the entire population was squeezed into the empty hardware store to watch. The fact that the seven bodies had not been removed and were still standing their ghostly watch from the front window added a touch of the macabre to the proceedings.

Pipkin opened the argument for prosecution, charging Jessup with terrorizing a town, with complicity in the murder of Parson Sloan and two other citizens who had been shot by his deputies while "resisting arrest," and with the direct murder of the cowboy Josh Speedwell through an act of illegal hanging.

Pipkin called Parmeter to the stand to testify with regard to the shooting of Parson Sloan. Parmeter told how Cooper and Bodine had come into his saloon on the day they arrived for the purpose of becoming Jessup's deputies.

"Did you witness the shooting of Parson Sloan?" Pipkin asked.

"Yes, I did," Parmeter answered.

"Please tell us in your own words what happened."

Parmeter told how both men began drinking, and how Cooper, intrigued by Sloan's hat, bet that he could shoot it off. Bodine took him up on the bet and the tragic result was that Cooper missed the hat and hit Sloan between the eyes. Afterward, he claimed it was an accident and Jessup made no effort to punish him for what was, clearly, murder.

"Mr. Parmeter, was Jessup in the saloon at the time?" Pipkin asked.

"Yes."

"Did he make any effort to stop Cooper from shooting?"

"No, he did not."

"Thank you. No further questions."

"Mr. Parmeter, you were in the saloon, weren't you?" Sam asked.

"Yes, I was."

"Did you make any attempt to stop Cooper from shootin'?"

"No."

"Why not?"

"For one thing, it wasn't my place. And for another, I was afraid that if I tried to stop him, he would turn on me."

"Thank you. No more questions."

Pipkin jumped up again. "If you were afraid, why didn't you go to the sheriff? He was right there, wasn't he?"

"Yes, but in somethin' like that, I knew he wouldn't help me," Parmeter answered.

"Thank you," Pipkin said. "Your Honor, prosecution calls Jarred Appleby."

Pipkin questioned Appleby about the murder of Josh Speedwell. Appleby explained how he had watched the young cowboy be placed on the back of a buckboard, then how the noose was slipped around his neck, and finally how the buckboard team was caused to dash forward, jerking the buckboard out from under Josh's feet and causing him to be hanged.

"Mr. Appleby," Sam said during his cross-examination, "when Josh Speedwell was hanged, was it by a large, unruly mob?"

"No, not really."

"Who was present?"

"The sheriff and all his deputies."

"How would you describe the proceedings?"

"Cold, calculating, mechanical, and frightening," Appleby said.

"Have you ever seen a hanging you considered legal, Mr. Appleby?"

"Yes, I have."

"How would you describe it?"

"Well . . . cold, calculating, mechanical, and frightening," Appleby said, realizing that he was using the same words of description.

"Then, in your mind, the only thing that was different about this hanging was that you don't believe it was legal?"

"I know it wasn't legal."

"But it was prescribed by the court, wasn't it?"

"By Jessup's court."

"But it was a court. It was not a mob lynching," Sam insisted.

"I suppose you could call it that."

"Thank you. No further questions."

As Jessup refused to testify in his own behalf, the case was over except for summation. Sam stood up and faced the jury that had been selected from among the townspeople.

"Gentlemen of the jury, the defendant, Charles Jessup, is not the kind of man you would want as a neighbor, or a friend, and certainly, not as an enemy. He is a man who has lived for many years by the gun, and there is no doubt in my mind that he has killed many men. But we are not tryin' him for livin' by the gun nor for killing many men. We are bringing him to trial for some very specific charges . . . as an accomplice in the murder of Parson Sloan, and for the murder of Josh Speedwell.

"If that is all we can find to try him on, then I've got some bad news for you. You can't find him guilty of that. He is no more an accomplice in the murder of Parson Sloan than is Parmeter. Both were present at the time of the shooting, but that is all. Neither of them pulled the trigger, caused the trigger to be pulled, or encouraged Cooper to pull the trigger.

"And as for Josh Speedwell, all you have to do is recall the testimony of Jarred Appleby to see that it wasn't murder, it was a court-authorized execution. And, gentlemen of the jury, whether you agree with that court's decision or not . . . it was court-authorized. But, what court? you might well ask. I will answer you. It is the same court we are in now, gentlemen, for according to Mr. Pipkin, the prosecutor in this case, the very legality of what we are doing now is based upon the establishment of a court in this town by Sheriff Charles Jessup. We cannot find his court illegal without finding ourselves illegal. We can't have it both ways." Sam looked over at Jessup, who was now smiling smugly. "Jessup is guilty of a lot of things . . . but he isn't guilty of the charges that have been filed against him today."

Pipkin, who had thought perhaps that Sam Slater would mount a listless defense, sat at the prosecutor's table for a full moment, stunned by the effectiveness of Sam's argument. Finally, he stood up and walked over to address the jury.

"Gentlemen of the jury," he said. "Mr. Slater has, indeed, given us something to consider. He has said that we cannot find Charles Jessup's court illegal without finding ourselves illegal. And there is merit to his argument, for, in the final analysis, we must be certain that what we are doing is not only legally, but morally right.

"Can we use this court to try Charles Jessup? And if this court finds Jessup guilty, and sentences him to death by hanging, can we carry out that terrible sentence without permanent damage to our legal status as a civilized community, and to our immortal souls?"

Pipkin crossed his arms to study the jury and saw that, to a man, he had their rapt attention.

"The answer to that question is . . . yes. We can act as a court. Because you see, gentlemen, the court itself is not on trial here. What is on trial here is the perversion of that court, as was perpetrated by one man . . . Charles Jessup. You can find Jessup guilty of perverting the court to commit the murder of Josh Speedwell, while at the same time you affirm the sanctity of the court itself. Therefore I ask you to find a verdict of guilty. Thank you."

Lem Miller, still in his military uniform and

now acting as judge of the court, turned to the jury. "The jury may now retire to deliberate," he said.

It took the jury a half hour to find a verdict. During that deliberation, Pipkin came over to talk to Sam.

"I was very impressed at the defense you put up for Jessup," he said. "I thought you would just roll over."

Sam shook his head. "Hangin' someone is a serious business," he said. "Anyone who is involved in it, no matter what part of it, has to treat it that way." He nodded toward Jessup. "If he didn't get the best defense I could possibly give him, you people would carry the guilt of hangin' him to your graves. This way . . . if the jury finds him guilty . . . and if he is hanged, there will be no second thoughts."

"The jury is comin' back," someone shouted from the rear of the building, and everyone took their seats to await the verdict. When the jury was seated, Miller looked toward them.

"Has the jury reached a verdict?"

"We have, Your Honor," Suter said, stepping forward. "And I have been selected to speak for it."

"How find you?"

Suter cleared his throat. "To the charge of accomplice in the murder of Parson Sloan, we find the defendant . . . not guilty."

There were several gasps and groans of protest from those in the audience, and Miller, using a carpenter's hammer as a gavel, banged on the table several times for order. Jessup smiled, broadly.

"Maybe I had you all wrong, Slater," he said. "What do you say after this is over, me and you get together like I suggested when you first come here?"

Sam glared at Jessup.

"How find you to the second charge?" Miller asked Suter.

"To the charge of murder of Josh Speedwell, we find the defendant . . . guilty."

This time the audience erupted into cheers and applause and, again, Miller had to bang his gavel for quiet. Finally, with the audience silent, Miller cleared his throat.

"Thank you, gentlemen of the jury," he said. "You are now dismissed. Would the prisoner please stand?"

Glaring, now, Jessup stood.

"Charles Jessup, you have been tried by this court, established under the effect of martial law and presided over by me as the commander of the militia. This court has found you guilty of murder in the first degree and I therefore sentence you to be hanged by the neck until you are dead. Sentence is to be carried out tomorrow morning. Please escort the prisoner across the street to the jail. This court is adjourned."

As two men stepped up to grab Jessup in compliance with Miller's instructions, Jessup looked over toward Sam.

"Come around tomorrow, Slater. I'll try and do a fine dance for you," Jessup said.

Sam shook his head. "My job is over," he said. "I never watch the hangings."

"I see. It's just collect your money and go, is that it?"

"What money?" he asked. "Jessup, you never were important enough for anyone to put a price on your miserable hide."

"Then, I don't get it. Why did you do this? Why did you come after me like you done?"

Sam smiled. "Why, Jessup, I thought you knew," he said. "Sometimes a man does somethin' just for the fun of it."